Silver and Aconite

by

Tashia L. Fugate

A Prophecy of Blood and Flowers,
Book One

Cover Art by *Lea Schizas*

The Wild Rose Press, Inc.
PO Box 708
Adams Basin, NY 14410-0708
Visit us at www.thewildrosepress.com

Publishing History
First Edition, 2024
Trade Paperback ISBN 978-1-5092-5802-4
Digital ISBN 978-1-5092-5803-1

A Prophecy of Blood and Flowers, Book One
Published in the United States of America

Dedication

To my mother, whose love and excitement for reading motivated me to write this book. I am forever grateful for you and I am beyond proud to be your daughter.

Acknowledgments

Writing a book involved so much more than taking an idea and transforming it into words on a page and there were so many people that helped make that dream become a reality. The idea for this story bloomed years ago when I was jotting down character names and scenes for certain chapters with one of my best friends. Thank you, Jami, for listening to me read chapters out loud when they were only rough ideas and for always giving me your honest opinion on everything. We've always been a dynamic duo; Gus to my Shawn and Sean to my Nathaniel; Shyamalan and King.

Although the story got shelved and wasn't thought of again until now, I have to give the biggest thanks the big man upstairs for giving me the signal to pull it out again and finish it and that's just what I did. Thank you to Amanda for introducing me to author Brooke Taylor and thank you Brooke for sharing with me your knowledge of the writing world. Your help is greatly appreciated and won't be forgotten. Thank you to the Samantha's in my life that gave me the okay to name my heroine after you. The strength, courage and love you've both shown helped to shape her character.

Something crucial a writer needs are test subjects. Great friends that will read your book in its roughest shape. Thank you, Kim, for donating to the cause and reading my chapters. Thank you to my "manager" Amanda and to Robin for also reading my book. Thank you for all your invaluable suggestions and keeping me motivated. Thank you, Alissa and Kay, for believing in me when I wasn't sure I believed in myself. Thank you, Kesha and Kasey, for all your social media expertise and thank you to Mandy, Teresa, Nicole and Jenn and all my other amazing work friends that listened to me babble about this book every day. I appreciate all your suggestions and insight throughout this writing process.

A huge thank you to The Wild Rose Press President/

Editor-in-Chief, Rhonda for answering all my questions and thank you to my editors, Ally and Tami, my social media manager Samantha and to all the other wonderful staff at The Wild Rose Press for making it possible for this book to be brought to the world. Thank you to Pat for going out of your way to help me make that final decision.

Thank you to all my family and friends for your enthusiasm throughout each day that I was glued to my laptop working on edits. All of you kept rekindling my excitement and motivation and I appreciate every positive word of encouragement you gave me. My four nephews keep me young; my dad keeps me wise; my mom keeps me dreaming and my sister Candice makes sure I never give up.

And now, last, but certainly not least I want to thank my husband, Thomas. Thank you for always being my biggest supporter. Thank you for understanding my passion for creating even on the days when I stayed in the craft room for hours trying to finish "this last paragraph". Thank you for cooking when I was focused on edits and thank you for helping keep the house in order when I was lost in my imagination. You give me strength to push through when things get tough and the courage to go forward when the future seems scary. Thank you for listening to me and letting me bounce ideas off you.

Finally, I want to thank you, my readers. Thank you for giving this book a chance!

Prologue

Living is sometimes harder than dying. To choose to fight and push through the callings of death rather than succumb to them is a decision that no person can make for someone else. We must want to live. We must fight as hard as we can, not just for ourselves, but for those we love. It is the people that we cherish more than life itself that make it all worth it. Life is hard, and sometimes sacrifices must be made, but we push through and live. It is days like today that break us down. Today, dying feels easier.

Samantha closed her eyes as she tried to catch her breath and clear the blurriness from her vision. The warehouse was so close, but still so far away. Large raindrops fell in slow succession as she lay on her back on the hard floor of the abandoned school. Lightning streaked through the dark, cloudy sky after every heart-pounding crash of thunder rumbled through her chest. She wanted to scream, to cry out and let go of all her frustrations, but to release them would be the first step to letting go, and she could not do that yet. She was doing the right thing; she knew that now.

With another attempt at a deep breath, Samantha brought herself up into a crouched position. Standing was harder now, and her head spun as she tried to balance herself. She pushed back on the bile that threatened to come up from her stomach. It had been how many days since she ate anything? She couldn't remember. Time over the past few days seemed strange and distant. She let her breath out slowly as she stood using the aged bricks of the old school's walls for support.

Her favorite pair of black running shoes were soaked and caked in mud and grass. Two drops of black fell into the pooling rainwater. The drops started to spread out like dark red branches of a tree. She was dying, but she wasn't dead yet. There was still some fight left in her, and she had to keep going.

She let go of the wall and wiped the blackened blood from her nose with the sleeve of her gray hoody. The wind pushed against her, and with each gust, it reminded her of just how weak she was. Without finishing what they started, she knew she would die. This was her only chance to live.

Samantha stared sadly into the dark path she had just traveled. The ones she loved most were back there and were no doubt finding her note by now. They had tried everything they could think of, she knew that, but there was no other way. This was the only choice, and she had to do it alone and hoped she would be powerful enough to fight what she was supposed to become. Her body was weak, but her mind and her soul were strong.

The rain stung with every hit to her feverish skin. It was dark where she stood in the old school, but the light from the blood moon lit the wet, gray stones on fire. The remains of the old building were hardly recognizable as a school anymore. It had been there since the sixties, but she could almost see where desks must have been arranged around what remained of the large brick fireplace. She imagined happy smiling faces, eager to learn from their teacher, but just as eager to get back home to their families.

Samantha's heartbeat was slow, and everything around her moved slowly with it. She turned her head up to peer through the open roof of the school to glare at the moon. The connection she once shared with it was forever tainted. The moon was once something that fascinated her, always glancing at it when she would leave work on a clear night, but now it held so much more meaning. She gritted her teeth in frustration and anger. What once brought so much joy now brought on feelings of fear and hatred.

She pulled her long, soaking wet hair back away from her face in a tight ponytail at the base of her neck. Enough time had already passed since she left their hiding place back at the cabin. Time was running out. In the distance, the top of the warehouse peeked out over the next hill. It was now or never. With one last glance at the moon, she left the old school building behind. The gravel road led straight to the warehouse. She knew this because she had been down this road before.

With clenched fists, Samantha mustered up all the fire she had left within herself and marched on to meet her destiny. The word sat heavy in her mind. *Do we make our own destiny, or has fate already planned it all out for us?* This fueled her determination more. She would play into their plan, but she would not be their puppet. This ended tonight.

Chapter 1

Deacon took refuge in a dark alley to catch his breath. He recognized where he was. One of the buildings next to him was a café and the other a barbershop, and thankfully, they were closed at this time. He needed a moment to rest, but he didn't have that luxury. They would catch up to him soon enough, and he would be surrounded. He laid his throbbing head back against the cool bricks that made the back wall of the café, hoping to get some relief. His deep brown hair was darkened to black from the rain that had soaked every inch of him. His face was pale from the loss of blood, and his chiseled features were darkened by the five-o'clock shadow of his beard.

He slowed his breathing in order to focus on his next move. The town of Glenwood was smaller than where he grew up, but it was still big enough for monsters to hide around every corner and for them to go unnoticed by the masses. It was nearing dawn now, so the streets and sidewalks were filling with the early risers and daily commuters. Headlights of passing cars lit up part of the alley, and for a moment, he could be seen. Their bright lights shone through the fog and flashed in his light blue eyes for a second or two.

An older lady spotted him standing in the alley. She clutched her umbrella tighter and snarled her nose at him as if he was the monster. He was breathing heavily, and his clothes were torn in various places. She eyed him suspiciously and muttered something about transients before she crossed the momentarily empty street to the sidewalk away from him. He didn't blame her for what she thought of him. He knew what he was.

The chances of evading his pursuers this time seemed futile. Straining hard, he tried to hear any sign they were getting close. It was stupid of him to get caught in the first place, but there was nothing he could do about that now. The storm and the increasingly busy streets of the town jarred his focus. The bullet was still lodged in his back, weakening him. They must have laced the bullet with a toxin. He would have healed by now if it was a regular bullet. A sickening feeling in the pit of his stomach made him bend at his waist. An icy sting that was trying to bring him down coursed through his veins.

Dawn was vastly approaching, and the sun would eat away at the darkness, which would make it easier for him to be found. Taking a deep breath, Deacon willed himself to stay calm and focus. There had to be nine or ten of them at least, and they'd brought dogs with them.

"Wonderful," he said to himself through clenched teeth. Each breath he let out was strained. They were surely closing in on him. He needed a plan, and fast, or he would be right back where he started.

He shoved his pain and feelings far away as he pushed from the wall in a dead sprint just as one group of men were minutes away from his position. It was tiring to run with the rain soaking his clothes, weighing him down, but he moved out of the alley onto a small back road. The road was used during the day to unload trucks of merchandise, but right now it was empty. He was rounding a corner, when an intense light exploded to his right, and he slid on the wet earth and gravel. He blinked furiously and shook his head trying to regain his sight while he picked himself up from the ground. Someone had launched a flash-bang arrow at him. Panic tried to spread through him as he realized they were closer than he thought. He had to keep running. If he stopped now, it would mean recapture.

Dogs snarled in the distance. Their vicious barking grew louder as they closed in on him. The sound of bullets pinging off the buildings and garbage bins echoed around him. They were using silencers, so their aim would not be true. With each footstep he took, his pulse pounded in his ears. Before he was even one hundred feet away from the alley, a faint clicking sounded behind him, and two taser prongs dug deep into the skin of his back, stinging like fire ants.

The two electrically charged probes sent energy throughout his body, tightening his muscles, and scrambling his brain in seconds. He hit the wet ground hard, splashing muddy water up around him. He tried to push through the fog in his mind, but he couldn't breathe, and his body was not cooperating. With all the force he could muster, he reached up with a muddy hand and grasped the wires at his back.

A deep and angry sound forced its way through his clenched teeth as he was able to relieve his attacker of the gun, stopping the volts of electricity from entering his body. He ripped the barbed prongs from his flesh while the man at his back approached him quickly to try and land another attack. Deacon threw out one of his legs, catching the man hard at his abdomen. The kick sent the man toppling into a stack of old crates piled up beside them.

Deacon endured more than he thought he could handle. A large part of him begged him to stop, to just lie down and let them finish him, but the rest of him urged him to keep moving. Breathing even harder now, he staggered for a moment but willed himself to run. He made his way around the buildings and out onto the main street. The area was becoming increasingly full of people, all carrying umbrellas or holding newspapers over their heads to shield themselves from the rain. Some of them curled their lips in disgust at his ragged appearance. He was soaking wet and muddy from the night's run, but they walked on without a second glance. If his appearance reflected how bad he felt, he could not blame them for their reactions.

He kept with the crowd for a little while and said a small prayer that his pursuers would not bring their fight into a crowd of witnesses. They had secrets too, and they would not want the people of this sleepy town to start asking questions. Rounding a corner onto a vacant side street, he came up to what smelled like a bakery. Deacon pressed himself against its front wall. He watched as most of the crowd disappeared into shops and other buildings in the area. Warm light spilled out of the bakery windows to his right. The light shone on the black asphalt along with the glowing neon lights of a sign saying the bakery was a twenty-four-hour place.

He bent over and rested his palms on his knees and bowed his head. Reaching out with his hearing once more, he located another group of men along with dogs barking and whimpering as the men wrangled them back into their cages. The dogs were still in hunt mode, but they were calling off the search for now. The anger in the man's voice as he spoke to someone else chilled Deacon, but the other man's response was drowned out by the bang of a bullet being fired. The sound of it echoed in Deacon's ears as he fought the wave of nausea that washed over him.

Withdrawing himself from their conversation, he let out a slow breath of relief, but he wasn't out of hot water yet. He pushed away from the building, but he couldn't push back the pain anymore. The adrenaline was starting to wear off, and the icy poison was leaching its way into his chest, and soon it would be in his heart. The muscles in his legs carried him a few feet toward the bakery's front door before he collapsed. The sidewalk was cold and hard as the rainwater splashed up around him. He lay flat on his stomach, and every inch of him hurt.

A woman gasped as she neared him but was tugged away by the man at her side. The movement splashed dirty water on his face. He lacked the strength to react.

"This town's going to the dogs. Drunks lying everywhere. Ridiculous. Let's go, Margaret." The man's long raincoat billowed behind them as they hurried in the opposite direction. The early morning fog blurred their silhouettes until they were gone.

He closed his eyes hoping it would make the burning stop and help to clear the black dots that danced behind his eyelids. The raindrops pelted his body like liquid bullets fired from a machine gun. He needed to get to his feet, but before he could try, a hand touched his forearm. Anger and hatred lay heavy on his chest at first as he assumed the worst, but the touch was warm, and the smell of sweet bread filled his nose. A soft voice soothed him as his body was gently turned.

Darkness threatened to take him, when he heard a second voice. He willed his eyes to open, but they would not. He thought they were talking to him, but he couldn't understand what he was hearing. Every muscle in his body tightened and released. The only thought in his mind was he must be hallucinating. A thought surfaced as he began to lose consciousness. *Is this how it feels to die?*

Chapter 2

Samantha was too stunned to move as she gaped at the man lying before her, the umbrella she was about to open forgotten at her feet. She wore her black work shirt with "Jake's Bakery" embroidered on the front with khaki pants and tennis shoes that were quickly becoming soaked by the rain as she stood rooted to the spot. A voice pulled her from her frozen state.

"He's bleeding. Is he dead?" asked the other woman as fear tightened her pretty features. Dark red spiraled through the rainwater as it pooled underneath his body.

Samantha squinted through the rain at Rhonda who wore the same work uniform as she did. They had just clocked out for the day and were about to go home until they spotted him lying on the ground not moving. Rhonda was a little shorter than she was and a few inches wider in the hips. She kept shifting her weight from foot to foot as her teakwood-brown eyes bounced from the man on the ground, then up to her car that was parked not a few feet from the bakery. She chewed on her lip with nervous energy. Samantha knelt with caution to inspect the man.

"Don't touch him!" Rhonda snapped as she inched closer to Samantha and tried to pull her back. Rainwater slid off her umbrella and dropped on the man's face, causing him to stir. "Ah! He's waking up. Call the police!" Rhonda urged her with an elbow as she pulled her long braided brown hair over her shoulder.

He blinked slowly as he peered up at them. His brows knitted together as he shook his head. Samantha's long coat was soaking up water as she examined him more closely. Something about him was familiar, but she couldn't place him. He might have been someone she passed on the street or a customer of the bakery. She would have remembered if he had been one of her patients from the emergency room where she also worked when she wasn't at the bakery, but there was nothing but this feeling inside of her.

His features were handsome in a rugged way, and his icy blue eyes seemed to peer right into her soul. "He needs a doctor," Samantha finally said as she took his pulse. It was so shallow she could barely feel it. His skin was hot to the touch like he had a fever. *He's lost so much blood!*

"Well, call an ambulance, Doctor Obvious, and let's get the hell out of here," Rhonda said in a sarcastic but scared tone.

"You know how the ambulance service is around here. They won't get here in time. This man's going to die if we don't help him. Help me get him in your car." Her palms rested on the slick fabric of his shirt.

"No thank you, ma'am. We are not putting a dying, stranger man in my car. I do not care how good-lookin' he is," Rhonda responded, shaking her head, and moving back to the safety of the bakery doors. She had a Kentucky accent that always got thicker when she was stressed or mad. "And what do you think you can do for him? You are not a surgeon. You're a nurse. You help the people who do things like this." Rhonda stopped talking when she heard the man murmur something.

"Samantha?" the man asked in a faint voice. His gaze held recognition like he knew her too. His hand slid across her cheek as he tucked a loose strand of her bangs behind her ear. Her long, brown hair twisted and curled slightly over her shoulders as it got wet from the rain. His fingers were warm against her cool cheek. "You're here." His voice was hoarse with pain, and he was barely keeping conscious. His hand dropped slowly back to the wet concrete.

"How does he know your name?" Rhonda's wide eyes narrowed with concern. "Do you know this guy?" She covered all three of them with her large umbrella to shield against the rain as she got a better view of him.

"I think I might. I don't know. Something's familiar about him," Samantha considered as she made up her mind. "Help me get him to my apartment."

"Are you crazy?" Rhonda eyed her, pulling back. "No way am I—"

"Rhonda!" Samantha raised her voice an octave. "Either help me, or I'm doing it alone. We have to help him."

"Ugh!" She stomped a low-heeled boot on the sidewalk, causing some water to splash up on her pants, and dug her keys out of her pocket. "Fine! But if he wakes up and kills us both, believe me, I will be so mad at you."

Rhonda ran to her nineties dark blue Grand Prix and slid into the driver's seat. The car wasn't anything fancy, but it was good on gas and ran fine. Samantha learned sometimes you must take what you can get and go on. Once she paid off her medical bills from her accident and finished paying back her student loans, she would have her own car. A chill ran up her spine as the wind picked up. A blanket of gray clouds blocked out the rising sun. She was exhausted, but she had to do this. She was no surgeon, but she hoped she knew enough to save his life.

"I hate you so much right now. You know that, right?" Rhonda spat as she got out of the car that she had parked closer to the sidewalk where the man lay.

"I know, I know," Samantha huffed. "Take his legs, and I'll lift under his arms."

The two women worked together to get him into the backseat of the car. Thankfully, there was no one else on the street or else they would have had a lot of unwanted attention. Jake, the bakery owner, was no doubt still finishing the inventory check and would not be done for a while.

"This is a very bad idea." Rhonda huffed as she slammed the car door closed.

"It'll be fine." Samantha swallowed. "Let's go." They loaded up and caught their breath for a moment. Her apartment was within walking distance from the bakery, so they would be there in no time in the car. With a sigh and another eye roll, Rhonda maneuvered the vehicle out onto the street and turned right on Highland Avenue.

This road mostly consisted of apartment buildings, with a few shops scattered here and there in between. A few people were hustling to get in their vehicles before getting drenched by the rain. Samantha spotted her three-story brick building surrounded by perfectly maintained bushes, with flowers on every window ledge. She thought about her little apartment as she hoped she had what she needed to fix this guy. Her stomach twisted with nerves as uncertainty filled her mind. She stole a quick glance at the backseat where the man now lay. He knew her, and something about him eased her nerves.

Rhonda parked around the back of the complex, which put them closer to Samantha's building. Her apartment was on the second floor, and thankfully, there was an outside elevator that had been installed the previous year to help the elderly residents and anyone else needing assistance up to their rooms. Samantha hoped they wouldn't run into anyone since this would be hard to explain. Getting him into her apartment might be harder. He had to be over six feet tall. The lines of his chiseled body showed through what was left of his soaking wet T-shirt.

He hadn't said another word since he spoke her name. He was in and out of consciousness for the entire drive. He groaned and gritted his teeth through every erratic start and stop of the car. His heavy frame made it difficult to move fast as they drug him from the backseat. They lost their grip on his arms and legs with every corner they turned. Samantha's skin was hot from the exertion as her wet clothes clung to her body in the small elevator. "Come on, I need you to stand. Just a little."

"I'm about to drop him." Rhonda adjusted his arm over her shoulders but was quickly losing her hold on him. Samantha rushed to unlock her door and helped to tug him inside. Thankfully, he wasn't completely deadweight, or they never would have made it this far.

"Lay him on the bed." Samantha straightened her comforter out and helped to position him face down as gently as they could.

"This is a terrible idea." Rhonda stepped back from the stranger, shaking her head.

"You don't have to stay. I can do this myself." Samantha darted around her apartment, locating all the necessary equipment. She stripped her wet jacket off and tossed it aside.

"I can't leave you by yourself."

"I'll be fine. I'll call you in the morning." She washed her hands and gloved up before taking her position next to the bed.

"Samantha…this is crazy."

"He doesn't have long. I have to do this now." She cut the length of his T-shirt with scissors and pulled the tattered fabric from under his body. She noticed blood on his jeans as she tossed the tattered shirt in the corner of her bedroom.

"I hope you know what you're doing." Rhonda left the apartment, leaving her alone with him.

Her heart hammered in her chest as she took a steadying breath. The smell of rubbing alcohol mixed with the metallic tang of blood-soaked gauze. The scent filled the room. She dried and cleaned the wound on his back and realized that he had been shot. He turned his head toward her, showing the tightened features of his face. "What happened to you out there?"

His hands slid across the surface of her bed as he attempted to rise up. He grimaced from the movement and rested his hands near his head.

She slipped her fingers into the round grips of a hemostat and prepared herself to remove the bullet. "I'm so sorry about this." She inserted the metal tips into the wound carefully.

He groaned through gritted teeth as every muscle in his body tensed until she withdrew the instrument. His fists tightened around handfuls of her comforter. The bullet fragment was unlike any regular bullet she had seen before. The remains of its shell had carvings on it, but without seeing the whole casing, she couldn't make out the design. She cleaned and bandaged the wound as he breathed heavily. His body shivered under her touch.

"Everything's going to be all right." She kept her voice low as she worked. As if her words soothed him, he released the blanket. His breathing slowed as his eyes danced behind closed eyelids. Stitching wounds was something she excelled at. Her fingers moved swiftly until the cuts on his arms were patched and covered in clean gauze.

He was going to be okay. He had to be. She eyed her cell phone that was lying on her dresser, but blocked out her thoughts that ran wild in her mind. Her chair creaked as she rested against its smooth wooden back. The crimson that had covered her white gloves was slick between her fingers.

Her heart hammered in her chest, but she did it. This was the right thing to do. The muscles in his back rippled with his deep breathing. His brow furrowed as the muscle in his jaw clenched, and then he was out.

****

Samantha stood at the foot of her bed and scanned the scene before her. With the bloody gauze and all the scattered first aid materials, it resembled one of the emergency rooms at the hospital where she worked. Slowly, her eyes settled on her bed where her patient slept. His color was already returning to normal. The only sounds in the room were their slow breaths and the faint ticking of the clock on her nightstand.

There was something familiar about him, but she could not place him in her memory anywhere, which at times was normal for her. She was suffering from amnesia that she had gotten from a car crash five years earlier. Nothing of her past life ever came back to her no matter how many therapists she saw or what techniques she tried. She had given up on her past and had been working hard to make her future something to be remembered. She sighed as the man's chest rose and fell with every breath.

A thought ran through her mind that he might be someone from her past, and that was why he seemed so familiar to her. He had said her name, so he knew her somehow, and how odd it was that he ended up in front of her workplace just minutes before she was due to leave. She never lost hope that she would unlock the secrets of her past, and at this point, she was willing to bet on anything.

His strong hands rested softly at his sides. Samantha traced a path with her eyes from the tips of his fingers up to his muscular arms and over his broad shoulders. He took up a little over half of her full-size bed. It was a miracle that she and Rhonda managed to get him here. Rhonda had been so good to her over the years. Their personalities clicked the moment they met right after Samantha woke up in the hospital. At the time, Rhonda had been working in housekeeping, so she was around every evening and would always strike up a conversation with her.

When Samantha left the hospital, Rhonda took her in until she could get back on her own two feet. There were bound to be many questions to answer later regarding her decision to help this man. No doubt Rhonda had fallen asleep with her phone in her hand, just waiting for the police to call her saying she was killed by some strange transient man. Rhonda was always a little paranoid, but this time she had a right to be.

The risk of bringing him here to her apartment like she had was a big one to take, but she couldn't let him die. As this thought crossed her mind, she eyed her Louisville slugger that she kept next to her bed for emergencies. She was technically only a nurse that worked in the emergency room, but she helped with enough procedures to know a thing or two about bullet wounds. She hoped he would wake up soon so she could talk to him and ask questions, but that idea scared her. She quietly tiptoed around the bed to retrieve the bat. *Just in case.* She was alone here with him, but the feeling she got from looking into his eyes wasn't a bad one. She wasn't in any danger. All she could do for now was wait.

His face was serene despite how rough his night must have been. "What happened to you out there?" Samantha asked aloud not expecting to get an answer. She walked to his bedside so she could recheck his pulse. She slid her fingertips across the exposed underside of his wrist. It was still slow, but steady and getting stronger. Relief washed over her. He was going to be all right, but just to be entirely safe, she would drive him to the hospital as soon as he was able and have him examined by the doctor on duty.

Tiredness washed over her. The adrenaline of the night's adventure had drained away. Yawning and stretching, Samantha headed toward a plush lounge chair that sat against the wall opposite the bed. The sun was beginning to shine brighter now that the rain had stopped, and the clouds began to dissipate. The sun's rays warmed the room with its orange glow as if a warm blanket were being wrapped around them.

She would have to go to work at the hospital in a few hours. Working two jobs to pay for her little apartment and cover the bills was sometimes hard, but she hoped she wouldn't have to work both places forever. She would do what she had to for now. Samantha snuggled into the soft cushions of her favorite armchair and watched the man sleeping in her bed, until she was overtaken by drowsiness and fell into a deep sleep.

Chapter 3

As Deacon slept, his mind drifted back to the night's events through his dreams. He was sneaking around in the dark trying to get the information he needed from the hunters he followed to that place. They were gathered in an old factory building from what he could tell. He had been so close, but they caught him. He tried to run out the way he snuck in, but found the passage blocked. He was hit hard by one of the bigger men and was kicked to the ground. Before he could fight back, he was hit by a stun gun and then another and another until he could no longer think as he passed out.

The voices he'd heard that night were running together in his head. The dream took on a nightmarish tone. Colors spun and melted together. Everything went dark, and there was a man stepping out of the shadows behind him as he ran. The dim lighting glinted off something long and metallic. A rifle barrel was aimed directly at him. In a flash of fear and pain, the rifle ignited in a fiery blast.

Deacon jolted upright as the nightmare images faded away. His eyes darted around the room as he tried to get a grip on himself. His bandaged body caught his attention. The thick tape stuck tightly to his skin as he picked at the corners to remove some of the gauze to show smooth, unharmed skin underneath. He must have been right about the bullet. It had to have been laced with wolfsbane. The scent of silver and his blood drew his attention to the nightstand that stood next to the bed. On top was a bowl that held the remains of the bullet alongside gauze and other first aid supplies. Since the bullet was removed and the wound cleaned, his body was healing itself. As he got up from the bed, he also realized that he was very naked.

Next to the stand, thrown into a corner, was what remained of his clothes. He knelt beside them to see what he could salvage. The clothes were still wet and were in tatters and covered in bloodstains. He sighed as he rolled his shoulders, feeling how tight they were. His muscles still ached as did his back. He was healing, but not as fast as usual.

A creaking sound behind him brought his attention to the wall opposite where he stood. Slightly hidden in the shadow of the room, a woman slept soundly in a chair. A fuzzy memory of her face surrounded by rain came to the front of his mind. It was her eyes that had triggered the memory at first. He couldn't believe what he was seeing, but it was her. The rhythm of his heartbeat quickened.

Their memories surfaced in his mind. Her name was Samantha. The two had a past together, but he wasn't sure that she remembered him. Realizing again that he was still naked, he pulled on his wet jeans from last night and slipped his feet into the cold and soggy tennis shoes. They were still caked with mud, but they would have to do for now. He examined the dark blue fabric that had been his shirt but discarded it back to the floor, since it had been cut from its bottom hem through the collar.

Deacon stepped quietly toward the chair. Samantha was curled into herself like a ball and held a wooden bat loosely in one hand. This brought a small grin to his face. It had been years since he had seen her. He began to wonder how she could be alive when everyone else he knew was dead.

A sound like that of a shotgun blast broke through his thoughts, and he tensed. Stepping to the room's small window, he peered out onto the street. A beat-up Chevrolet truck was turning the corner. Smoke trailed from the vehicle's tailpipe. He released his breath. The truck's exhaust had backfired. This whole situation had made him on high alert.

The sound of a yawn and another creak from the overstuffed chair brought his attention back to Samantha. She was waking up, and he wasn't ready to have this conversation. He was down the creaking steps of the fire escape within seconds and stepped around the building's edge. Before he was completely out of sight, he stole another glimpse of her bedroom window. He would see her again soon. Now that he knew she was alive, he would do as he'd promised. He would protect her, and with that thought, he was gone.

****

Samantha yawned and was startled by the bat clanging against the wood floor as she lifted her arms to stretch. She stood and snatched up the bat only to realize her bed was now empty. Her heart dropped as she searched the entire apartment, but there was no sign of him anywhere. Only his muddy shoe prints remained. Returning to her bedroom, she noticed his discarded clothes had been sifted through. In the corner of her eye, her sheer white curtains moved in the gentle breeze coming from outside.

She was sure that window was closed last night. *He*

must have left through it, but how? she thought. *How is he able to move after what he went through last night?* She closed the window and cursed herself for falling asleep. As she faced her bedroom, she sighed at the thought of cleaning this place up.

A man's voice broke the silence of the apartment, and she jumped. The deep voice crackled but was still recognizable in the speaker box by the front door. "Samantha. It's Michael. Buzz me in," said the voice through the speaker.

She rubbed her dry eyes.

Michael McCray. He was the youngest son of the wealthy McCray family that owned much of the town. She sometimes wondered what he was doing dating her, when so many other women showed him interest that matched his world far better than she ever could. Doing a mental head slap, she realized how long she had been asleep. She jogged to the speaker box. "Oh, Michael. I'm so sorry. I overslept," Samantha said while in her mind she wondered how she was going to explain the operation scene that was her bedroom.

"Forget it." He chuckled. "The coffee shop was packed anyway. I brought coffee..." he sang, "and pastries..."

Samantha rolled her eyes. Michael never failed to show up with coffee and pastries every morning. He was always trying to spoil her, even though sometimes she didn't want all his fancy gifts. She took a deep breath, and with a shaky finger, she buzzed him in.

It would only take him a few minutes to get to her door. Without any time to clean, she pulled the sliding doors together that separated her bedroom from the rest of the apartment, concealing the mess within. She caught a quick glance of herself in the full-length, standing mirror in the corner of her living room. She took another deep breath. A shower was needed, and the sooner the better. She was pulling her hair into the black hair band she always kept on her wrist when there was a knock at the door.

Samantha shook away the nervous feeling and put on a broad smile as she opened the door. "Why, hello there, Mr. McCray," she teased as she gazed into his mahogany-brown eyes. He was taller than her with an athlete's build. His long arms and legs were lean and toned as he clutched the to-go carrier that held their coffees and a bag of donuts from her favorite café.

She could get lost in the darkness of his eyes, but sometimes they took on a possessiveness that she wrote off as him being overprotective. His eyes were so deep brown they were almost black in certain settings. He smiled down at her in the way he always did when he saw her before kissing her cheek and walking past her into her small living room.

He sat the food and drinks on the bar that separated her kitchen and dining area from her living room. As soon as she closed the door and turned to meet him, he was directly in front of her. She turned her eyes up to him as he slid his hands over her sides and down on her hips. She grinned up at him as he slipped the thumb of his right hand under the bottom of her T-shirt and caressed her stomach. "I had you on my mind all night," he whispered in her ear.

"You did, did you?" she asked, pulling him into her as she wrapped her arms around his neck. She was tall for a girl but still had to stretch her arms a little so that she could reach around him.

"Oh yea." Michael kissed her neck slowly up to behind her ear, sending a chill through her body. She breathed deeply in response to his lips as they moved across her skin. The scent of his rosewood cologne mixed with coffee and sugar filled her. "I could show you just how much," he said in a husky voice in her ear as he put his palms flush against the door to Samantha's back, pinning her there.

"Hmm…" Samantha considered as she put her finger to her chin and tapped it in a thinking gesture, avoiding his dark gaze. "I think I'll just take the coffee and donuts." She ducked under one of his arms. "You know how much I hate cold coffee." She laughed as she dug into the bag of treats. A Bavarian cream filled was on top with her name on it.

"You cut me deep." Michael sighed with his hands dramatically placed over his heart. He joined her on the other empty stool next to the bar. Samantha noticed how his jeans and T-shirt tightened against his muscles as he reached for his coffee. His smile oozed confidence.

Samantha laughed through a big bite of donut as he swiped a drop of chocolate from the corner of her mouth and licked it from his finger. "Delicious." He gave her a hungry look that had nothing to do with pastries. Michael was handsome and had always been so patient and understanding with her. They had bumped into one another as she was leaving the hospital years ago after having the stitches removed from her head injury she had sustained in her accident.

Samantha had assured him that she appeared far worse than she was feeling. Michael had been so sweet and charming as he helped her into Rhonda's car that day. He was careful not to touch her bruised and scraped arms. Many times during her recovery, he would check on her, and from there, things started to blossom with their relationship. She thought she loved him at times, and sometimes she was unsure. She did not want to make any bad decisions.

His black hair was usually cut short, but today, it curled around his ears slightly, and his bangs hung loosely above his eyes. Samantha liked being able to run her fingers through the smooth strands every chance they were together, snuggled in front of her small television set on the rare days she was off from work. He was a practical choice for her, but she had never said she loved him. Not him or anyone else either, she realized.

"Why the long face?" Michael asked. "That's your favorite breakfast food." He lifted her chin to see her eyes. "Everything okay?"

She side-glanced at him as her mind wandered back to her encounter last night. The man she saved had eyes so different than Michael's. They were the eyes of a stranger, and yet there was a connection to him like she'd never had with anyone else. He seemed so familiar that it irritated her to not be able to place him.

Michael's voice interrupted her thoughts. "Uh, oh. I know that look." He set down his coffee and leaned back on his barstool. "What's on your mind?"

He was always asking her this question. If she was quiet for too long or stared off into space, she was thinking of all the things she couldn't remember. Seeing a child with their parents or when certain holidays came around, she would find herself in this state. Samantha just stared at him for a long moment, trying to decide if she should tell him about what happened last night.

Michael interrupted her train of thought. "What's

that smell?" he asked as he got up from the barstool to move around the apartment.

Samantha's mouth went dry as cotton. She sat her donut down on a napkin and slid off her stool to cut off Michael's path to her bedroom. "What smell?" she asked, trying to sound oblivious to the lingering traces of blood and alcohol.

"You mean you don't smell that?" Michael moved around her to further investigate the source of the smell. "It's pretty strong." He grasped the knobs of the double doors leading to her bedroom and pulled them open.

"I can explain that." Samantha pushed past him into her room. "I was about to tell you about this." She gestured at the mess that was her bedroom. It was hard to read Michael's expression. His eyes and the firm set of his mouth showed a hint of concern, some curiosity, and a whole lot of suspicion. They stood in silence for a few seconds.

"Tell me about what?" He ran a hand through his dark hair, pacing the small room. "Whose blood is this?" Samantha picked at her fingernails as she tried to find the words to explain. He stopped moving around and was now staring at something behind her. She turned, following his line of sight until she saw the tattered remains of a shirt.

"It's complicated, but I can explain." Samantha pulled the bedding off her bed. "There was this guy and—"

Michael interrupted by taking the covers from her and throwing them down on the mattress. "What guy?" His nostrils flared, and he breathed heavily as he glared at her. He had never taken that tone with her before, and she did not like it.

Her posture stiffened as heat flooded her cheeks. She managed to speak to him through clenched teeth. "I saved a man's life last night, and if you would be so kind as to stop interrupting me and let me explain, then you might understand." She ripped the covers and pillows off the bed again and threw them on the floor with a heavy thump. She filled her lungs with a deep breath and released it slowly as she tried to control her temper while glaring back at him.

Minutes passed as they stared at each other until Michael broke the silence. "Okay, I'm sorry." He moved away from the bed and leaned on the ledge by the window, arms crossed over his broad chest. "What happened? Tell me everything." He stared at her without showing any emotion. Samantha hated to be interrupted, and it really got under her skin when people assumed things about her before letting her explain. He was acting as if she were a child who had done something wrong.

Once Samantha was in control of herself again, she began the story, rattling off the words quickly. "Last night when me and Rhonda were leaving Jake's, we practically fell over this guy lying on the sidewalk. He was hurt badly, so we brought him here, and I fixed him. He was bleeding out, Michael, I had to help him. He would have died." She searched his face for any sign of emotion, and when he didn't move or speak, she continued. "I planned to take him to the hospital once he was able to be moved, but I fell asleep, and when I woke up, he was gone. I had to, Michael. He wouldn't have made it to the hospital."

Michael pinched the bridge of his nose and sighed. "Dr. Quinn, Medicine Woman." He shook his head and rubbed his hands over his eyes. "You know he could have killed you, right? Who's to say he wasn't some low-life *dog* that was being hunted down?" Michael stood up, and in one fluid motion, he knocked everything off her nightstand onto the floor with his arm. "That was foolish and careless," he finished saying as he pointed to the contents scattered across the floor. Light glinted off the bullet fragment as it rolled against the wall.

Samantha's jaw dropped, but she stayed rooted to the spot where she'd been standing as she watched Michael move around the room. "Why are you acting this way?" she asked. "I'm perfectly fine. I was just trying to help someone."

"Did you recognize him?" Michael asked, ignoring her question.

Samantha paused, deciding to leave out the part about the stranger knowing her name. Michael wouldn't understand, not right now at least. He needed time to cool off, so she lied about recognizing him. It was in that moment that she realized the man had been awake and moving around the apartment while she slept. He could have killed her or robbed her at any moment, but he hadn't.

Samantha took another deep breath. Realizing she had been doing that a lot lately, she said, "It may have been foolish and, yes, even careless, but he was dying, and at the time, it didn't matter what kind of a person he was. No one deserves to die like that. I made a choice, Michael, and I know it was the right one."

He kept his eyes trained on the floor when he huffed, "You should have at least called me."

"There was no time for that." She closed the space between them and took his hand in hers. "I just reacted and did what I thought was right." She leveled her eyes with his, but they were distant. She suspected he'd be worried, but she had no idea he would be this upset. "Michael?" she asked when he still didn't respond. "Why are you acting like this?"

"I have to go." He dropped her hands and stepped away from her. He left her standing alone in her bedroom with tears in her eyes, slamming the front door as he went. She jumped at the sound, and a tear slid down her cheek.

Chapter 4

Night shift at Glenwood Memorial Hospital was usually calm but was busy last night. Sebastion could not wait to get into his apartment, take a shower, eat, and then sleep. It didn't have to happen in that order, but that was his plan. He already had his door key in hand when he got off the elevator that opened to the fourth floor. His complex wasn't fancy, but it wasn't a dump, so he was happy with it. The rent was cheap, and it was a quiet place. Most of his neighbors were older people who he hardly saw, so it would suffice until he could afford something better.

His chestnut-brown hair curled around the edges of the blue beanie he wore to keep the cool outside air from chilling his ears. His heavy, brown jacket was too warm inside the complex over his blue hoody and scrubs. The jacket hem stopped just below the waistband of his light blue scrub pants. Sebastion was two inches above six feet tall and still had a runner's build even though it'd been weeks since he had done any cardio.

His deep brown eyes were tinted a deep crimson that varied depending on the lighting and his mood. Tonight, they were dark and slightly bloodshot as his heavy eyelids drooped in exhaustion. He could already feel his soft bed as he neared his door. He knew double shifts were a bad idea, but he had agreed to do it anyway. At least now it was over.

Sebastion yawned and squinched his eyes together as he fumbled to fit the key into the lock. After a couple of tries, the key slid into place, and the lock turned over with its familiar clicking sound. He pushed the heavy wooden door open and shuffled into his foyer, closing the door behind him. Any other time, he would have noticed that he wasn't alone in the apartment, but he was asleep on his feet. He had just decided to skip the food and the shower and go straight to bed, when he heard someone speak from the shadows of his apartment.

"Someone missed their beauty sleep," Deacon informed him from the small dining area that was the room to the right of the foyer as he switched on a light.

Sebastion's eyelids popped open. All the drowsiness he'd been feeling went away in an instant. He jumped and almost flipped himself over his computer chair that was pulled out from his desk. He furrowed his brow in annoyance at who was sitting at his table with a smirk on his face. "Deacon?" He picked up the computer chair and put his messenger bag onto it. "What the hell, man? Are you trying to give me a heart attack? How'd you get in here anyway?"

Sebastion pulled off his heavy coat and hoody as he entered the small dining area. The room was barely big enough for a small round table which only had three chairs that didn't match, but it was enough for him. He placed them over the back of the smallest chairs with the shake of his head. His hair stood in different directions after pulling off the beanie and tossing it onto the table. He crossed his arms as he turned to Deacon, waiting for his response.

"You really should lock your fire escape window when you leave," Deacon answered.

Sebastion rolled his eyes and moved into the kitchen to rummage through his refrigerator. Sleep would have to wait. The light inside the fridge and the cool air stung his eyes as he pulled out two containers of an opaque green dessert and a pack of chocolate sandwich cookies. Sebastion raised one of the snack packs and offered it to his guest, but Deacon shook his head in response. After grabbing a spoon from a drawer, he joined him at the table.

"That's disgusting," Deacon said as Sebastion dug into his food.

"You broke into my apartment, again, and about sent me to an early grave. You don't get to talk about my food, okay?" He popped another cookie into his mouth. "This is growing-boy food," he tried to say as he sputtered cookie crumbs from his lips.

Deacon rubbed his hands over his eyes. "Right." He sighed with a shake of his head. "Eat up." He still wasn't feeling his best but knew this couldn't wait. He had to talk to Sebastion about what he had found out from the hunters. After leaving Samantha's apartment, he stopped by his place for a quick shower and a change of clothes. All his wounds were healed except for the bullet wound. He applied a fresh bandage as best he could before he came here. "I need some information," Deacon said, getting to the point of his visit. "I had a little run-in with some hunters I've been tracking."

Sebastion froze with his spoon inches from his face. He sighed and shoved the jiggling, green stuff into his mouth and chewed it slowly as he regarded him with concern. Deacon had dark circles under his eyes. His brown hair was styled in a pretty boy sort of way that always made Sebastion wonder what products he used to keep it that way all the time. Sebastion kept his hair in a buzz cut, but he had been so busy these past few months he never got around to getting it cut. The black leather jacket Deacon wore over a navy-blue T-shirt contrasted harshly against the pale tone of his skin.

Sebastion had known Deacon for the better part of five years now, and he knew messing with hunters could mean trouble, especially if the person doing the messing was a werewolf. Sebastion's family dealt with hunters and werewolves over the years, and although he managed to stay out of major trouble with both parties, he did get into a few scrapes from time to time. One of those times, Deacon had saved his life, and he never forgot it.

"Knowing you," Sebastion said as he finished his last dessert cup in one large bite, "a little run-in is shortchanging it a bit. Am I right?" He leaned back and basketball tossed his spoon into the sink with a clank.

After Deacon went through the whole ordeal, Sebastion just stared at him incredulously. "Do you have a death wish?" he finally asked. "What were you thinking?"

Deacon stood up from the table and walked toward the fire escape window that he previously came in through. He pulled back the dark blackout curtain and peeked out at the street before replying. "I was thinking if I didn't follow them, I wouldn't know what I know now."

"Which is what?" Sebastion asked.

"Something's coming." He turned from the window and faced Sebastion. His face was tight as he narrowed his eyes. "They found information on a prophecy. There's a weapon or ritual that can take out werewolves and any innocent people that get in the way. Werewolves and humans, Sebastion. I need your help to figure it all out before they find whatever else they need, or more people are going to die."

Sebastion stood facing Deacon as he recalled the hardest night of his life. He had both hands in fists around the collar of his scrub top. The fabric pulled down a few inches, revealing a silver cross necklace around his neck. His parents had been killed over a year ago by a group of hunters they suspected were searching for information. There was evidence of a struggle, but they were outnumbered when the hunters found them. Sebastion feared it was werewolves that had killed his parents at first, but after examining the wounds, it was clear what killed them. Werewolves didn't need guns to kill.

The cross had belonged to his mother. It was Sebastion and his uncle Oscar that had found them, but they were too late. Oscar was a hunter, but he went by a code. His team only took out the monsters that broke the treaties that were in place to make sure there was no unnecessary bloodshed. Sebastion had taken the necklace from his mother's cold neck, and together, they buried his family. The ones responsible were never found.

"Are they the hunters that killed my parents?" Sebastion's throat went dry, and tears stung his eyes.

Deacon took a breath and eyed Sebastion. They were like brothers. They had been through a lot together. Emotion was something Deacon never learned to deal with. He hated seeing the pain in his eyes. He pushed the feelings down into himself, turning them into fuel for the fire that kept him going. His anger was how he expressed his feelings, and that usually ended with him breaking something or fighting, but Sebastion was different.

"I think so." Deacon finally answered Sebastion's question. "I tracked most of the group back here to Glenwood. They had your father's journals. I tried to sneak them out, but that plan failed."

Sebastion licked his lips and chewed them for a moment before kicking one of the kitchen chairs against the table. It slid in place and then toppled over onto the floor. He laid his hands on the cool tabletop and dropped his head. Deacon stood silently as he made sense of this new information. Losing your parents the way Sebastion did was hard enough, but to know their killers were living in the same town as you made it that much worse.

After a long moment, Sebastion straightened and ran his forearm across his eyes and breathed a couple of deep breaths before facing Deacon. His face heated, and the burning in his eyes worsened. He tightened the muscles in his jaw as he clenched his teeth together. "What can I do?" he asked, more determined than ever to hunt down the people that took his parents from him, and take them out. Whatever they knew he would know soon enough, and he'd beat them to whatever it was they were looking for. That was a promise.

****

Samantha's lungs burned as a stitch formed in her side. She enjoyed her morning walks to the hospital, but today she couldn't be late. As the second hand on her wristwatch ticked closer to the start of her shift, her anxiety worsened. A bead of sweat dripped into her eye before she could wipe it away. She breathed deeply to slow her heart rate.

She arrived barely on time for her shift. Rhonda

stood next to the time clock, tapping her pen furiously against her clipboard. "Rhonda!" she yelled as she jogged over to clock in for her shift.

She closed the distance between them just as Rhonda let out a sharp breath and propped her hands on her hips like a mom angry at her kid for missing curfew. "Do you know how freaked out I've been?" she shouted. "I almost called the cops twice last night from worrying about you. You are not allowed to do that to me again, you understand me? My anxiety cannot take it." Her face flushed red under her tan skin as she crossed her arms when Samantha didn't say anything.

"I know. I'm sorry, but I'm okay, see? Not a scratch on me." She made a show of modeling her unharmed body.

Rhonda sighed and hugged her tightly. Their embrace filled Samantha with relief. They took care of people in worse situations every day, but she understood how last night's events were far from normal. Samantha was older by eight months, but Rhonda was like the older sister that always tried to mother hen everyone. She pulled back from the hug and squeezed her hands.

"So, did your patient do okay in surgery, or do I need to get my shovel?" Rhonda held a serious face before her lips spread into a wide smile.

Rhonda was like a whirlwind of emotions. She could go from sad to mad to happy in the span of five minutes. She was a mess full of anxiety, but she loved her. "No. No shovel needed." Samantha faced the time clock and swiped her badge. With a beep, the time clock read 7:33 AM. "Crap!" Samantha exclaimed. "I'm late again. Bonnie's going to write me up today, I just know it." She checked behind her, half expecting her supervisor to pop around the corner, layoff notice in hand.

"You're off the hook," Rhonda said as they made their way to the emergency room wing of the hospital. "Bonnie's out sick today. Flu or something. I don't remember."

Samantha's face relaxed. "At least something's working out in my favor this week."

"You saved a man's life and got away with being late, again. What's not working out?" Rhonda held a swinging door open for her, allowing her to take the lead. "So, did you find out about that guy? What was familiar about him? Do you know who he is?"

Samantha picked a foam cup up off the blue and tan squares that made up the hallway floor and tossed it into a nearby waste can. "He left before I could talk to him. I fell asleep."

"You should've cuffed him to the bed. I know you still have those handcuffs from when you and Michael dressed up as cop and prisoner last Halloween."

Samantha laughed a little at her attempt to lighten the mood. "Those were plastic, and don't even get me started on Michael."

That piqued Rhonda's interest. "I take it he wasn't as receptive to your heroism as I am?"

"No, he sure wasn't," she said as she entered the code to open the emergency room doors. "I have never seen him so mad. He blew up as if I cheated on him or killed someone rather than saved a man. I don't know what his deal is. I know it was risky, but I knew that man wouldn't hurt me. Michael wouldn't let me explain. He just took off."

The emergency room was empty as they entered open space. Samantha was thankful for that. She was too tired and was getting another of her migraines. There were no patients in the beds and only a couple of employees already sitting at their computers. She sat down at her desk and rubbed her eyes.

"Another headache?" Rhonda asked.

"Yep." Samantha turned on her computer monitor. The small black screen came to life showing a beach scene somewhere in Hawaii and a place for her to log into the hospital's system. Samantha wished she were on a beach somewhere. She had a lot of vacation time built up, but she always chose to save her money rather than spend it on trips. Michael offered to pay for them to visit Rome or Paris, but she preferred simpler dates rather than extravagant ones.

She and Michael were hugely different people, and at times she wondered why he was interested in her in the first place. She didn't feel like anything special, but Michael always tried, and she guessed that was all that mattered.

"Maybe you should see that doctor again," Rhonda suggested.

"No thanks," Samantha said, keying in her log-in credentials. "He'll just go on about my accident and how amnesia works, and I'm just not up for it."

Rhonda nodded and typed her credentials on her own computer. She was positioned next to Samantha in a row of other computers and chairs. "Is the medicine helping at all?"

"Not lately." Samantha massaged her temples before facing Rhonda. Lines formed on her forehead, and the corners of her mouth were turned down. "I'm fine though, really. If it gets worse, I'll go see someone else, okay?" Samantha hoped this would ease her concern.

Rhonda gave a small smile and a nod. "Okay." An ambulance pulled up outside of the outer ambulance entrance. Its flashing lights were visible in the shadowy carport.

"What if I never see him again?" Samantha asked, pulling Rhonda's attention from the ambulance.

"You'll see Michael again," Rhonda insisted. "He'll come around."

"Not Michael," Samantha said, wishing she knew the name of the man she saved.

"Who?" asked Rhonda. "The hot, almost dead guy?" Rhonda shrugged one shoulder and reached for a clipboard. "You never know. He might show up here today. The man really should be in a hospital."

"Are you doubting my skills?" Samantha grinned as she stood up.

"Remember we went to nursing school together. You have terrible bedside manners. We've not seen the last of him, I'd bet. I wouldn't mind seeing him again. Under all that blood and muck, he was hot. I bet he has a sexy name too like Adam or Channing."

Samantha rolled her eyes. "What am I going to do with you?"

Their laughter was interrupted as a man walked in through the side doors that led to the waiting area. He was escorted by their triage nurse and held a thick towel around one of his hands. Blood was soaking through the white fabric as he was moved to one of the beds. "Time to go to work." Rhonda nodded toward the wounded man.

They filled their pockets with ink pens and other supplies and got to work. As Samantha pulled on a pair of pink, latex gloves and headed over to bed one, she thought about what Rhonda had said. She didn't believe in fate but was willing to put her faith in it for the moment. That was a lot to hope for, but she couldn't give up. Something in her erased all doubt. The thought of unlocking her past gave her a boost of energy she didn't know she had but welcomed it all the same. The empty ER they had walked into was quickly turning into a terribly busy day.

Chapter 5

Hours had passed since Deacon left Sebastion's apartment. He couldn't stay at his place and wait to hear back from him. Not knowing was eating at him. The night the hunters had caught him, they tied him to a gurney that stood up next to a lot of intimidating medical equipment, and questioned him ruthlessly about stuff he didn't know. Between shocks of electricity, he could barely make out pieces of the conversations going on in a nearby room. They needed different things to complete a weapon, but if he understood correctly, they found the person that was the key to their plans. There were too many unanswered questions.

The people he passed on the street today nodded with smiling faces as if he were one of them. He couldn't be angry with the humans who avoided him this morning out of fear or disgust. His memory was full of faces that viewed him in that way. They didn't know what went on around them, and he hoped for their sakes they never found out. He returned their smiles with one of his own but didn't speak as he kept moving.

The sun was shining brightly on his face as the wind blew what was left of the storm clouds onto another city. He closed his eyes and breathed in the air. It held so many different scents that only his kind were able to notice. At times he wished he could be like the people he passed on the street. To be oblivious to all the real dangers would be such a relief, but that wasn't his life.

There was a vibration in his jacket pocket that broke into his thoughts. He pulled out the new disposable phone Sebastion had given him earlier that day. The display showed Sebastion's name above an answer or decline button. He slid his thumb over the green answer button allowing him to answer the call. As he brought the phone to his ear, he checked to make sure the street was clear before crossing to the other side of the road where he had been walking.

Several occupied benches were placed near the entrance to the building in front of him, so he jogged around the side and found an empty picnic table next to some trash cans and ashtray stands. A few small benches sat empty in a line by the building. He checked to see that there was no one within earshot of him before speaking into the small speaker of the cell phone. "What'd you find out?"

"I've been online at the library for hours, and you wouldn't believe how much false werewolf lore I found. I blame the movies myself." Sebastion's voice came through the speaker. "I didn't have a lot of luck online, but I snuck into the archives and found a few things. Check your messages. I sent you some pictures."

Deacon heard a ding in his ear. The screen displayed three messages that held images he could click on to enlarge. The first had a dark picture of a scroll with frayed edges. At the top, there were four blood moons, and underneath each of the moons were symbols he didn't recognize. The second image displayed instructions for setting up equipment that was like what he saw at the hunters' base.

The third image showed a sketch of a half human,

half wolf figure on his knees. His eyes were squeezed together with pain on his face. The expression was all too familiar to Deacon. Standing behind the creature was a beautiful silhouette of a woman. She had her hand tenderly placed on the creature's shoulder. The woman's eyes glowed a fluorescent purple flecked with silver. Off to the right and behind the main parts of the painting was a group of men wielding weapons and grinning with satisfaction.

"Scary, right?" Sebastion asked.

"What does all this mean?" Deacon tilted his head at the strange symbols. His brows furrowed in frustration. "What do these symbols translate to?"

"From what I was able to decipher, they talk about a prophecy." Sebastion fumbled with papers in the background as he spoke. The phone dropped and was fumbled before his voice returned.

"It's a blend of ancient languages, so I'm having trouble with all the details," he said with worry starting to creep into his voice. "They want to create a weapon that can kill werewolves, but we're not talking just silver bullets and aconite poisoning."

Deacon was quiet as he listened to the silence on Sebastion's end of the call until he started talking again. "It's a human. The weapon is a girl. It talks about this crazy ritual about blood and flowers. This is some dark age stuff. The hunters you ran into, they don't really think this is possible, do they?"

"I'm afraid so," Deacon replied as his thoughts ran wild. The girl they want wasn't going to build something, she was going to be the weapon. "Let's hope they don't have her yet."

"We never get that lucky." Sebastion spoke through

a yawn. "We have to find her first, but this will be like looking for a needle in a haystack."

"There must have been something in your father's journal that helped them get as far as they have." Deacon spoke as he pulled the phone back to his ear and leaned back on the bench. A couple of men wearing scrubs walked by him and buzzed themselves into a side door. Deacon waited for the door to close behind them before he continued. "Would Oscar know what the journals contained?"

"I'm not sure." Sebastion yawned again. "I left him a voicemail earlier but haven't heard back yet. Hopefully, he'll know something."

Deacon clenched his teeth together, until the muscle in his jaw tightened, as he squeezed the backrest on the bench with his free hand. He knew the ruthlessness of hunters, but this group was not to be taken lightly. There was evil on both sides, werewolves and hunters. The werewolf packs that hunted and slaughtered innocents had to be put down. This was something he accepted as he got older. In his youth, he had joined a pack outside of his family because he thought it would keep his family safe, but as time went on, he realized how wrong he was. By then, however, he was too late.

"You still there?" Sebastion asked.

"I'm here. Just thinking about how things end up over time. This life we're in, it's—"

"Don't beat yourself up, man," Sebastion said. "Don't let your mind go there. We make choices, we learn from them, and then we go on. Terrible things happen to good people, but it's not our fault. We can't control everything, and you know I understand that mindset. If we stop this, then they won't have died in vain."

Deacon had made his choice to leave home years ago. He thought his new pack was the answer to everything, but their views and ideas turned out to be very different from what he was promised. The night he threatened to leave the pack, they made sure he had nothing to go back home to. Their alpha Kiren had his family slaughtered in front of him and would have killed Sebastion and Sebastion's uncle Oscar as well, but Deacon defied his alpha, and together with the help of Oscar's team, they barely escaped with their lives. Sebastion was right, but it was still hard not to feel hatred toward himself. His guilt was immeasurable.

Some days he couldn't stand to see his own reflection. Not every day was like that, but his guilt haunted him. A flash of Samantha's face came to his mind. She was a happy piece of his past that he never thought he would see again. He didn't know why, but in his soul, he knew she remembered him. She would be safer and better off if she forgot him entirely. Deacon wanted to find her and protect her, but if he really wanted to protect her, he would have to leave her alone. He couldn't drag her into this mess and risk putting her in harm's way.

"Sebastion," Deacon asked. "Do you know a Samantha Martin?"

"Uh, no. I don't think so." He seemed thrown off by the topic change. "I'm not good with names though."

Deacon described Samantha the best he could remember from the other night. Her appearance hadn't changed much at all now that she was older. Her beauty had grown with age. His heart dropped as he remembered the last day he had spent with Samantha all those years ago right before he left. They had fought, and she begged him to stay as she yelled at him about breaking his promise. He was still young then, and his head was full of ideas about his future. If he could go back to that moment, he never would have left.

"I know a Samantha that looks like that, but her last name is Walker," he spoke. "We work together, well, sort of. We're on different shifts, but it's at the same hospital."

"Which hospital?" Deacon asked. His heart skipped a beat as he leaned forward in his seat. His excitement churned in his stomach, leaving a bitter taste in his mouth. He shouldn't have asked. Knowing it would make no difference since he couldn't get her involved. He bit his inner cheek as he stood up from his spot on the bench and walked around to the front of the building.

"Glenwood Memorial. Do you not remember stuff I tell you sometimes? You must have selective hearing. Why do you ask anyway? How do you know her?" The annoyance in his voice was clear.

The building across the street caught his attention as he thought of a way to answer that question. Everything behind him was reflected in its large windows. A sign that read *EMERGENCY* in red caught his attention. His eyes moved to the name of the building. In dark blue letters that hung above the main entrance read Glenwood Memorial Hospital. "I have to go," was all he said before disconnecting the call.

Chapter 6

Sebastion's phone screen went dark after his call with Deacon ended. He laid it face down on the piles of papers that littered his once-organized desk. He wondered why Deacon was suddenly interested in Samantha Walker. Deacon wasn't an open book type of person, so there was still a lot he didn't know about him, but he trusted him and owed him his life. He picked up the printed picture of the scroll he took earlier. The images gave him a bad feeling, and he hoped his uncle Oscar would shed some light on the subject.

His thoughts were interrupted by a knock at his door. Startled by the sudden sound, he piled all his research together and stuffed it into his messenger bag. There was a second knock before he could make it to the door. He peeked out the peephole and was relieved to see a familiar face. He shook his head at his paranoia and pulled the heavy door open.

"Hey, Sebastion," Elijah Mitchell greeted him from the breezeway. Eli was a few years older than him and was a few inches taller. His wavy bronze hair was longer than he remembered, and his wild green eyes stood out among his strong features. Underneath his right eye, he had a crescent-shaped scar that was white against his tanned skin. On the day they first met, Eli explained how he got the scar. It was from a bar fight that he said he didn't start, but swore he finished it.

"Hey, Eli. Come on in." Sebastion gestured for him to enter. Eli used to work at the hospital with him, and that's where they were first introduced. Eli was hired a few months after he was but soon left to work at a different location. Sebastion couldn't remember right off which hospital he worked at now but shook away the thought as he closed the door.

The two had stayed in contact since, and luckily, they ran into each other at the library when he was there researching the prophecy. When he mentioned the scroll to him, Eli said he had some information at his house that might help. Eli was a history buff and knew a lot about dark age stuff. Sebastion was hesitant at first to tell him anything about the prophecy, but when his eyes lit up at the sight of the scroll, it was obvious he knew something about it, and right now, they could use all the help they could get. Eli didn't know any of this was real so it would be safe to let him help for now.

"What do you have for me?" Sebastion eyed his black backpack.

"You're looking pretty rough, bud." Eli shrugged off the backpack. "Getting enough sleep?"

Sebastion thought about the last time he slept, really slept. He had been awake going on three days, and his appearance showed every hour of that sleep deprivation. He dozed off for a few minutes at the library, but that was all the sleep he was able to get. "I picked up a double shift." He hoped he wouldn't ask anything more. His eyelids were sticking with every blink.

"Those double shifts will kill ya." Eli eyed him curiously.

"I know it." He motioned for him to have a seat at his table so they could get on with it. Sebastion was really needing the comfort of his bed now that his energy drinks were wearing off.

"First off, how did you say you came across this *ritual*?" Eli pulled a black folder from the backpack. "This is some crazy, really out of this world stuff."

Sebastion tried to remember the lie he had given him earlier. "I'm writing a research paper about the dark ages." The lie was flimsy, but he hoped Eli's love for all things history would outweigh his harmless lie.

"Right." He fanned out the ancient, yellowed papers on the table's smooth wooden surface. "The dark ages were dark. It was full of rituals and sacrifices. Especially this one." He pointed at one of the pages in the middle and slid it over for him to see. "The text translates to *The Prophecy of Blood and Flowers*. It says there will be the occurrence of four blood moons four months in a row, and this will set in motion a timeline."

The page before him was like the scroll he found, but this showed more details. The page showed a bloodletting procedure being done on a girl. The girl was the same as the image in the drawing he found, but without glowing eyes. Pain was sketched in her features as her blood leaked from various places on her body. Another section showed images of silver and wolfsbane being mixed with the blood over fire. At the bottom of the page, the girl was absorbing the new blood mixture. "What's supposed to happen in this timeline?" Sebastion asked as he imagined someone actually going through this transformation.

"The first blood moon is supposed to show the way to the chosen one," Eli read from his notes. "The second will bring forth a warrior and the first to be sacrificed. It gets difficult to decipher with that one, but the third one is straightforward. The blood of the chosen one must be tested by trials of fire, whatever that means, and the final blood moon is a counting clock."

Sebastion flicked his eyes from the paper to Eli. "A counting clock for what?"

Eli pushed one of the pages closer for him to read. "This page says if the final parts of the ritual aren't completed by the time the blood moon ends, the chosen one dies, and they must wait for the tetrad to come around again in a thousand years when another will be chosen. They tried this before but weren't successful. The texts don't say much after that. It's like all other records from that time were destroyed." Eli met his eyes. "You know we just had a blood moon last month and the month before that. We just need two more to make this ritual happen. That's some coincidence, wouldn't you say?"

Sebastion's eyes widened. He hadn't realized that there had been two blood moons back-to-back. If this information was reliable, then they were running out of time. He had to let Deacon know what he just learned.

"Don't get so freaked out. This is all just wild stories made up to scare people into following some religious cult or something. It's not like this is real, right?" he asked with a fox-like grin.

"Yea." Sebastion gave a small laugh. "Right." He tried to laugh off his worry, but it came out with more anxiety than he meant it to. He thanked Eli and mentioned he was going to get some sleep and said he'd let him know how the paper went, but that he might change topics. It was a darker path than he wanted to follow.

Before Eli left, he asked a final question. "You

didn't come across anything explaining how they would find the chosen one, did you?" Eli's expression turned so dark and serious that Sebastion found it odd, but Eli smiled and said, "Hypothetically. I would hate to be in her shoes." The laid-back laughter returned.

"Nope," Sebastion said. "No idea."

"I guess we'll have to keep digging." Eli shrugged his wide shoulders. "Catch ya, later."

When Eli was gone, Sebastion closed the door and leaned against it as he thought of who the chosen one could be. He truly had no idea, but he and Deacon had to find her first, whoever she was, and hopefully before the third blood moon. This whole situation just got a lot worse. The clock ticking on his living room wall matched the beats of his own heart. How much time did they have left?

****

Eli's smile turned to a sneer as he jogged down the stairs. The ground level of Sebastion's apartment building was empty. He pulled a cell phone from his pocket and flipped it open so he could make his call. The phone was in its third ring as he reached the sidewalk. There was silence at first when someone answered, and then he heard a man's voice come through the speaker.

"This better be important," the deep voice commanded. The annoyance in his leader's tone was evident.

"I think we have a problem with Sebastion." Eli spoke calmly and straight to the point. "He knows enough about the prophecy to cause problems, but he says they don't know how to find the girl."

Wind from the passing traffic ruffled his hair as he waited for his chance to cross. He smiled at the lady in a silver BMW who slowed and waved him across. His black Yamaha was parked behind the complex. He glanced up to Sebastion's floor. If only he could go ahead and end him, that would keep Deacon from finding out anything else. He was wise enough not to question his leader, but if he had his way, they'd wipe Sebastion and Deacon out. He didn't understand what was so special about either of them.

"I was under the impression that he was not a threat. Was I mistaken to have put you in charge of keeping him on the path we want him on?"

"You weren't mistaken." Eli ground his teeth as he tried to keep his anger in check. "He only knows what I let him know. He trusts me, but his loyalty lies with Deacon. He'll do anything to help him now."

The man sighed on the other end of the phone. "I'm losing faith in you, Elijah. This has gone on too long. They will find the chosen one, and when they do, I expect you to know as well, and when you find her, I want you to bring her to me."

He knew not to argue. To question his alpha would only get him killed or worse. "We will find the chosen one, and she will be brought to your feet before the hunters get to her," Eli said through gritted teeth. His chest rose and fell with heavy breaths of anger.

"I know you will," his master's voice spoke through the phone's small speaker. "I would hate to no longer have a need for your services, and we both know what happens to pups who've worn out their welcome, don't we?"

"We'll have the information we need soon." The calm in his voice gave him chills.

"For your sake, we'd better." The line went dead.

Eli stood by his bike for a moment longer as he digested those last words. Kiren was a merciless alpha, and he always kept his word. He both feared and respected him. He tucked the phone away with a growl of frustration. He hated being treated like a scrounging, mangy mutt. Even though he had climbed through the ranks of his pack all on his own and was now second-in-command, he still didn't matter. He deserved respect, and he would get what he deserved and more. It didn't matter who he had to kill, he would deliver the chosen one. A high-pitched barking drew him from his thoughts.

"Cocoa!" He heard an older lady say as she tugged on the leash she held in her hand. The leash was attached to a small Jack Russell dog that kept barking at him and pulling the small woman toward him. They had been walking by him on the sidewalk. "I'm so sorry," she said to him as she tried to get control of her yapping terrier. "He's never acted like this before." She shook her head and called the dog's name again.

"It's no problem." Eli bent down to face the dog as he continued to bark. "He must not like my aftershave." He stared directly into the dog's eyes. He smiled, showing his strong, white teeth, and allowed his green eyes to glow unnaturally. The dog stopped barking at once and retreated behind his owner with a whimper. He turned his still-glowing eyes on the woman, with a devilish grin. "I have that effect on most things."

The woman picked up her dog and backed away from Eli. Her pulse quickened at the sight of him. Her fear gave him a wicked energy as she took off down the sidewalk. His mouth salivated when he thought about how her beating heart would taste if he ripped it from her chest. He was confident he would get what he wanted, and Sebastion would be the one to give it to him. One way or another. He climbed on the bike, causing it to sag a little under his weight. He pulled away from his parking space and merged into traffic while a plan brewed in his mind.

Chapter 7

Deacon pulled his eyes away from the Glenwood Memorial Hospital sign and scanned the area and all the faces of the people that milled about around him on the sidewalk. Part of him hoped he would see Samantha's face among them, but he knew better. Getting her involved in his current situation would only end badly for them both, and he couldn't do that to her.

Flashes of Samantha's red and tear-streaked face from his past flashed to the front of his mind at that moment as he decided what to do. His chest tightened at the memory of how much sadness she and his sister suffered when he left all those years ago. The right decision would be to leave this area right now and not risk being seen by her or, worse, being seen with her.

If the hunters knew about Samantha, they could use her as leverage to draw him back in again, and this would land them both six feet under. He leaned his head back as a black cloud passed over the sun, blocking its rays for a few seconds. It was a cool day, but the sun warmed him when it reappeared from behind the large cloud.

He would avoid Samantha for now, and hopefully when this was all over, he could find her again and make everything right. If she didn't remember him, maybe that was for the best. Before he could turn around, a cool breeze shuffled a few fallen leaves around at his feet, and it snaked its way through his jacket, causing his skin to chill. He caught a familiar smell that froze him where he stood.

He dared a glance in the direction of her scent. The sweet aroma stood out among the crowd of people nearby, so he knew exactly where it came from and to whom it belonged. His eyes met Samantha's, and her gaze held him in place, not letting him breathe or do anything else but stare back at her. Although they were some distance apart, the details of her beautiful face were unmistakable. Her dark blue scrubs complemented her tan skin.

She was shadowed by the covered port that was attached to the hospital's main entrance, but he could trace every angle of her face with his eyes. Her long brown hair was pulled back into a ponytail that drifted lightly in the wind. Her eyes were trained on him as her lips parted and her eyes widened.

Quickly, Deacon turned his back to her and tried to walk away casually, hoping she hadn't recognized him and that she would go back inside the hospital, and all would be okay. Every fiber of his being wanted to turn back and go to her. He wanted to see how she was and give what they had together a second chance. If he was hunted, he couldn't endanger anyone else. He thought of Sebastion and cringed. It wasn't right to bring Sebastion into this either, but it was too late for that. He could be more involved than they knew. If the hunters knew about his parents, then they would have to know about him too.

Sebastion might know a lot about the things that go bump in the night, but that didn't make him any safer. If anything or anyone got to Sebastion, they would use him and then dispose of him. The thought of Sebastion or Samantha being killed because of him made him heat up with anger. Deacon cleared his mind of all thoughts and chanced a glance behind him to see if he was being followed. He spotted her at once several feet behind him as she started to pick up her pace.

Dread washed through him as he knew what he had to do. He had to lose her now and hope she'd forgive him later. Turning forward again, he pushed himself to run faster. If there hadn't been so many people around, he could have lost her in no time, but that would draw too much attention, and it didn't seem like the crowd would be thinning out any time soon. He could use the crowd to his advantage and slip around the corner of the next building that came up.

Deacon was at a full run as he strained his hearing to gauge how far back Samantha was. She kept up better than he thought, but he was widening the gap with every foot that pounded on the pavement. He was nearing the corner of a building that led into an alley between a white-walled pharmacy and another building he didn't recognize. The distance between them was wide enough for him to disappear. He pictured her sad face again, and he almost slowed down, but he pushed the thought away and turned fast around the corner of the pharmacy, almost taking out a passerby as he did.

Once he cleared the corner, he surveyed the area, and seeing that no one was around him in the shadows of the building, he used the windowsills that stuck out from the wall to begin his climb to the roof as fast as he could. He was thankful all the shades were drawn tightly against each window, so no one inside could be surprised by him peering in on them. The last thing he needed right now was to have the police involved. In seconds, he climbed the full three levels of the building and lifted himself up and over the roof's ledge so that he was out of sight from the ground below.

The roof of the old pharmacy was black but had lighter, blotchy areas here and there that had been bleached out by the sun after years of exposure. Water puddled in various places that were left over from the recent rainstorms. He was barely winded from the run, but he breathed deeply, trying to stop his thoughts from lingering on Samantha. The air smelled of wet asphalt on a muggy day. He focused on that smell as he watched a few birds take flight from their perch on the shiny metal of the building's air ventilation units.

After a few long minutes had passed, he was in control of his thoughts. He lost her, and hopefully, she gave up and went back to the hospital. If she was on the clock, she had to go back to work before they missed her. He hoped this was the case, because he wouldn't be able to hold himself back if he saw her again. He wanted to see her more now than he ever did before, and if fate kept landing him at her feet, he was bound to give in to it.

With some deliberation, Deacon slowly leaned over the roof's ledge to see if anyone was below him. The alley was empty, and he couldn't hear anyone walking close by. In a way, he was disappointed that she wasn't down there waiting for him, but he shook the thought away as he jumped up on the narrow ledge that ran around the building's roof.

There wasn't much that he truly feared in this world, but now the list was getting far longer than he could handle. With another deep breath, he stepped off the ledge and dropped the three stories down onto the hard concrete below without a sound and disappeared into the crowded street.

****

Samantha was ready for a break from the hustle and bustle of the emergency room. All morning she found herself eyeing the clock until she was finally getting to take it. The fluorescent lighting inside the hospital was bothering her eyes more than usual today, so she welcomed the shade that enveloped her as she stepped through the front doors of the hospital. The automatic door slid closed behind her as she took in a breath of fresh air. She liked to sit in the designated smoking area around the side of the hospital and listen to gossip or just watch people until it was time to get back to work. She wasn't a smoker herself, but she enjoyed having the company.

She was about to make her way around the building when she spotted him on the sidewalk. She did a double take and couldn't believe her own eyes. Time slowed down as the cool breeze blew up around her, ruffling her hair. Her eyes grew wide as she gaped at the sight before her. What were the odds that she would see him again today? Last night, he was nearly a corpse, but today, his stance was strong. The man she dug a bullet out of twelve hours ago would not be in any shape to walk around this easily. There was no way it was him, but there he was.

Unless this man had a twin, which was highly unlikely. She caught a glimpse of the side of his face at first until he turned his focus to the ground. His body visibly tensed up. His eyes slowly made their way to hers. She thought he was handsome before, but after seeing him now, she was stunned. The bright sunlight highlighted his dark hair, showing its deep brown color with hints of natural highlights scattered throughout. The icy blue color of his eyes shone through dark lashes, pinning her in place. He quickly turned his back on her, breaking their unspoken connection.

It took her a moment to snap out of the spell she was under, but once her mind was clear, an unseen force pushed her toward him. This was her moment, and she was going to take it. Before she got a few steps closer to him, he took off down the sidewalk. *What is this guy's deal?* His pace quickened, and she matched it step for step.

She passed a few of her coworkers that were heading back inside the building. She smiled and nodded at them but kept moving. Right now, she needed answers, and the one person who she thought could give her those answers was starting to get away. No way was she going to let that happen again. She kept her eyes trained on the back of his leather jacket so she wouldn't lose him in the crowd. He stole a glance back at her, and she met his cool eyes.

With each moment their eyes met, she was that much more compelled to reach him. She wished she could catch him and be able to dive deeper into his eyes and find all her answers buried within him. She was gaining on him, but he broke into a run and widened the space between them. In that instant, a heavy sadness came over her. A knot formed in her stomach and a lump in her throat. *Why did he run?* This intense sadness threatened to close in on her like shadows smothering out the light. Her eyes stung, and tears threatened to gush from them.

She pushed the feeling away and bolted into a run after him. She gained on him, but he was so much faster than she was. Her breath quickened as a stitch formed in her side. She had to double her pace not to lose him in the crowd of people between them. Her legs burned with protest, but she forced them to go faster.

"This is ridiculous!" she managed to say aloud to herself through deep breaths. "What am I doing?" she growled in frustration as she pushed herself to run as fast as she could. People eyed her with suspicion as she ran past, but that didn't stop her. She was beyond them in a flash and kept moving.

The pharmacy grew larger in the distance. If he planned to lose her, then it would be around that turn. She was strong like a lioness running down her prey. A very out of shape lioness, of course, but a lion all the same. She would not be denied this victory.

Her head throbbed when she pushed herself further. She tried to ignore it, but a sharp pain shot through the center of her brain and surged through her body. She slowed her pace and tried to catch her breath by raising her arms in the air and putting pressure on her head, hoping the pain would subside. The pain only grew worse. She reluctantly abandoned her chase and headed back toward the hospital.

The closer she got, the worse the pain in her head became. Her skull hurt as if it was splitting open, causing black spots to dance in front of her eyes. She stumbled and swayed on her feet as she tried to clear her vision. *What is happening?* She had migraines before, but nothing like this. The sadness returned and began to boil within her, turning to anger. *This was all his fault!* She pressed her hands hard against her temples. If only he would have stayed there so she could just talk to him.

She didn't understand why she was feeling so emotional about this. The feeling was distant yet familiar, and it was because of him. He left her behind.

A blurred figure of someone came into her view as a man approached her. A fog she couldn't shake wrapped around her mind as the smell of cigars filled her nose. Her heart punched her ribs with panic.

"Miss? Are you okay?" he asked her.

His hand touched her arm, but she couldn't respond to him. She tried to take control of her legs and push past him, but the sharp pain surged again, bringing her down to her knees. The thin fabric of her scrub pants ripped against the rough surface of the sidewalk.

She blinked and focused on the man, but things were changing in front of her. She shook her head as if that would make the images go away, but it only made her stomach roll. He left her behind with such ease. Her breaths came out in gasps as her chest ached with a sadness so strong it racked over her body.

The more she thought about this feeling, the more it grew and twisted its way up into her throat. Her arms and hands buzzed with a tingling sensation that coursed through her muscles down to her fingers. A wave of dizziness tried to take over, and she bent forward and rested her weight on her hands and knees. The concrete sidewalk dug into the soft flesh of her palms as more figures moved toward to ask if she was okay. Her lungs refused to take in air.

Her mind moved far away from everything as she blinked tears from her eyes. Even the temperature of the air turned more like summer than the fall season they were in. She was no longer on a sidewalk in Glenwood. The sun shone brightly through trees that surrounded a small playground. The concrete turned to soft blades of grass below her. Its familiar scent tickled her nose as she ran her hand over its prickly surface.

Laughter in the distance caught her attention, and she raised her eyes back to the playground. A little girl was smiling and laughing as the wind caught her long brown hair on her descent down the bright blue slide that she was on. Before the little girl could hop off the slide, Samantha spotted another child. He was a little boy that couldn't have been much older than ten. He was beautiful with his dark hair and blue eyes. He was hanging from yellow monkey bars and doing flips with ease.

The little girl tried to keep up with her companion but stumbled and fell onto the ground, scraping her knee. She held her knee in her hands and began to cry. The child's pain was her own. More tears fell from her eyes. Entranced by the vision before her, she wished the boy would slow down and come back to the little girl. She couldn't bear it.

"Deacon," the little girl said in a faraway voice. "Don't leave me."

The little girl's pain ached within her. She was seeing herself. She knew that now. She spotted the boy as he ran back to her. "I'm sorry, Sam," the little boy spoke softly to her as he moved her hands from her little knee showing a dark red scratch. "I'll never really leave you." He stretched out a small hand to help her up. The girl smiled up into those familiar blue eyes of the boy. "You're my best friend," the little boy continued to say as he held her small hand in his. "Friends don't leave each other behind."

"You promise?" the little girl asked.

"I promise," he answered with a smile.

The scene before her turned gray. As it melted away, she realized what it was that she had just seen. This was a memory. One of her memories! Her vision cleared as she sat back on the sidewalk. She could still feel the grass, and the faint pain in her knee lingered a few seconds more until it and the vision were gone.

People were gathered around her, but she was still deep in her thoughts as she replayed the memory over and over in her head. Her lips spread in a dreamy smile as the sadness faded. A single name floated to the front of her mind. It belonged to the man she saved.

"His name is Deacon," she heard herself say aloud. Someone's hand squeezed her shoulder as a lady wearing a jogging suit bent down beside her.

"Who is Deacon, sweetie? Is he someone we can call for you?"

Samantha blinked as she stared at the woman. Her dark hair was tied in a low ponytail that swayed each time she moved her head. She realized she had drawn in a small crowd. Their worried faces loomed over her as her cheeks grew warm. She put on her best smile and hoped they would see she was okay. Some of the group moved on as the woman helped her stand.

"I'm okay." Samantha focused on being convincing. "I just got a little dizzy from the run. I'm fine."

"We thought you were having a stroke or something," the man to her right said. He pushed his round glasses up the bridge of his nose. "We saw your name badge, so we called the hospital. The lady at the desk said she'd send someone."

"Oh, no. I'm fine, really." Samantha tried to walk on her own but swayed from the dizziness. "On second thought—" She took in a slow breath and let it out. "—maybe I'll just sit down for a minute." She was falling

before she could say another word, and then she blacked
out.

Chapter 8

Sebastion was sure he had just fallen asleep when he was awakened by his phone ringing on his nightstand. Without opening his eyes, he fumbled around with his hand trying to hit snooze, only to realize he was receiving a call. He blinked his eyes a few times to clear his vision so he could read the small screen. Seeing that it was a call he needed to take, he pressed the green answer button with his index finger.

"Hey, Oscar," Sebastion said into the speaker, trying to sound fully awake. "Are you back in town?" He sat on the edge of his bed. His black-and-gray blanket was partially covering his legs still as he waited to hear his uncle's voice.

Oscar's voice was deep but clear as he spoke over a bit of static that came and went over the connection. "No, not yet." His uncle shouted over some noise in the background. "We'll be back soon. We're just finishing here." He listened patiently while his uncle spoke to someone else. When Oscar returned to their conversation, his voice was serious. "I got your message," he said. "Is Deacon with you?"

"No. Not now. Why?" He shouldered the phone and rubbed his eyes until spots of light flashed behind his eyelids.

"I did some digging here. This is a bigger situation than we realized. The stuff you sent me about the prophecy, it's very real, and it explains why your parents were killed. If the wrong people had control of this weapon, they could wipe out all werewolves. The good and the bad."

Oscar paused as Sebastion tried to understand. "What do you mean?"

"Has Deacon ever mentioned a girl from his past to you? Someone he grew up with?" Oscar asked. The static got worse for a second or two and then cleared enough for Sebastion to answer.

"No, I don't think so," he replied as he tried to remember. "The only girl he ever talked to me about was Samantha Walker. Well, he asked about Samantha Martin, but the girl he described to me sounded like this girl I work with. Her last name is Walker though. He just asked if I knew her. Who is she?" Sebastion worked his fingers to massage the tightness from his neck.

Oscar was silent for a moment until he sighed. "That's a story Deacon will have to tell you. It's not my place, but what I can tell you is this. The research your father kept in his journals were key to finding out who the chosen one for this prophecy is, and that's why your parents were killed."

Sebastion stood up from his bed and tossed the blanket behind him. "How come Dad never mentioned anything about this to me?" he asked. "How did you find out about it?"

"Your father knew how dangerous this information was, Sebastion. He didn't want you involved. I just found out myself. He must have thought someone was after him because he mailed a letter to me explaining everything. I'm sorry, but your father wanted you left out of it. He wanted to protect you."

"It's a little too late for that now." Sebastion paced around his bedroom trying to make sense of everything.

"Don't be angry with him, Sebastion. You know how protective he was with everyone."

"What did his letter say?" Sebastion parted the blinds on his bedroom window to glance outside before leaning his bare shoulder against the cool wall.

"The letter mentioned a family, a human family, that knew about werewolves. They were descendants of an old line of hunters that everyone thought had been wiped out years ago, but a few remained. Martin was the name they went by while they were in hiding, and they knew Deacon and his family." Oscar gave more instructions to someone else in the background before he continued. "Your father discovered the same pack of werewolves that killed Deacon's family also tried to kill the Martins, but one escaped. Although, I don't know the details of how she managed it."

Sebastion let all this information sink in before he responded. "Samantha Martin was the only survivor?"

"That's what your father believed. The bodies of her parents were found, but she never was. If Deacon believes this Samantha Walker is the same girl, then we must get to her before anyone else does. Kiren's pack will kill her, and those hunters will try to use her to help their cause."

Kiren. Sebastion's bones shook at the sound of the alpha's name. His was a face he would never forget. Kiren was built like a tank with long dark hair streaked with sun-bleached strands like ash. His eyes stood out in his mind. Kiren's were deep set and always glowed an unnatural yellow. His brows were sharp and menacing. A long scar ran down his left eyebrow and onto his cheek. His brown goatee faded to gray down onto his square chin. His perfect teeth had long canines, giving him an animalistic appearance even in his human form.

"Sebastion?" asked Oscar. "Are you still there?"

Sebastion snapped out of the memory of his run-in with Kiren and his pack. "I'm here."

"Find Deacon and the two of you find Samantha," Oscar instructed. "You can take refuge at my cabin. I should be there in a day or so, and we'll figure all this out. If your father's calculations were right, then the hunters will move on her tonight."

Sebastion furrowed his brow. He still didn't fully understand everything. "Why tonight?" Concern tightened his chest as the connection buzzed with more static.

"There will be another blood moon tonight, and this will make the third one in a row. They'll have to test her blood soon to be sure they have the right girl, and I'm starting to believe she is." Oscar's voice was serious.

Sebastion ran his free hand over his head and face as realization set in. Once upon a time, he thought the only thing he had to worry about was werewolves, and now things have gotten worse. He had cold-blooded hunters, evil werewolves, and a weapon of mass destruction to deal with. *All in a day's work.* His eyes drifted to the calendar hanging on the wall. He disconnected the call with his uncle and stared around his small apartment, wishing this were just a bad dream that he could wake up from.

That wasn't the case, and now he had to figure out how to tell Deacon about everything he just learned. That was one conversation he wished he could avoid, but worse than that, how are they going to explain all of this to Samantha? He had heard talk about her accident and how she has amnesia. It's one thing not to remember your family, but another to find out the reason no one came for you was because they were dead, and it was because of you that they were murdered. Sebastion closed his eyes and sighed as he bowed his head.

****

Rhonda couldn't believe her eyes when the ambulance drivers wheeled in an unconscious Samantha through the emergency room doors. "What happened?" She rushed over to them. Two EMTs pushed a gurney through the wide doors by the ambulance entrance.

"Some pedestrians that witnessed the incident said she was running and then collapsed," said one of the men that Rhonda didn't recognize. They transferred Samantha's body to one of the emergency room beds. "Her vitals are stable, and she's breathing normal. She's starting to wake up."

Rhonda leaned over her. Samantha moved her head from side to side and slowly blinked open her eyes. "Thank God! Are you okay? What happened?"

Samantha squinted and rubbed the space between her brows. "I'm okay. Really." She smiled at the ambulance drivers and sat up on her elbows.

"Thank you both. We'll take her from here." Rhonda walked around the bed and pulled the curtain closed, separating them from the men and the rest of the emergency room. She sat in the tan chair nearest the bed. The wooden legs scraped against the smooth linoleum as she scooted closer. "What happened?"

"He showed up, and I remembered him." Samantha sat up fully in the bed. Her eyes shone with excitement.

Rhonda grasped her hand and arched her brow.

"Who showed up? You remembered who?" She feared Samantha may have hit her head when she collapsed, but her eyes were clear, and there was no sign of any injuries.

"Our mystery guy." She smiled. "I saw him outside, so I chased after him, and that's when I remembered."

"Okay, so you're telling me about the almost-dead man from last night was outside the hospital, and you chased him down? Honey, did you hit your head?"

"No. I didn't hit my head. I know it sounds crazy, but he was here. I didn't believe it was him at first either, but he recognized me. I could tell in his eyes." Samantha quickly recounted the whole incident to her without leaving out a single detail. When she finished her story, a big smile spread across her face as if everything made perfect sense.

If Deacon was someone from her childhood, Rhonda wasn't sure contacting him was such a promising idea. "Samantha, I know you want to believe in this guy, but isn't it possible he might be wanted by the police or something? He did have a gunshot wound, and he did run away from you."

The smile faded from her face before she spoke. "I may not know the whole situation, but I know he means no harm to me. I just know it. I can feel it in here." She placed her hands to her heart. "Maybe he just doesn't know how to approach me, and I scared him off."

"Always the optimist." She shook her head. "Okay. We'll say he's a good guy for now, but next time you see him, how about you get me, and we'll talk to him together just to be on the safe side, okay? Promise?"

Samantha smiled and nodded. "I promise."

As the girls squeezed each other's hands, the sound of hooks scraping against the metal pole that held up the curtain caught their attention. Rhonda turned to see Dr. Franzin, the evening physician, as he walked toward the exam table. She stood up to make room for the good doctor.

Dr. Franzin was an older man. He was tall and slim with receding salt-and-pepper hair. His dark blue eyes gleamed through wire-frame glasses that set on the tip of his nose. He stood with a medical folder in his hands as he skimmed through the pages before he spoke.

"Miss Walker, it's a twist to have you on this side of the doctor–patient dynamic," he joked as he walked to her bedside. He tucked the folder tightly under his arm and took a penlight from his white physician's coat. He shined the pinpoint light into Samantha's eyes and had her follow it while he nodded and returned the pen to his pocket.

Samantha followed his instructions but flashed her a *help me* look every time he scribbled in the folder.

"Can you tell me what happened?" Dr. Franzin shuffled through a few more pages within her file.

Her eyes shifted hesitantly from Dr. Franzin to Rhonda and back to the doctor before answering. "I went for a run on my break and must have gotten too hot. I passed out and woke up here."

Rhonda eyed her suspiciously as she realized she was altering the truth a bit.

"Uh, hunh." Dr. Franzin jotted down more notes on one of the pages. "That can happen."

"I feel fine now though," Samantha said enthusiastically. "Am I okay to go?"

Rhonda rubbed at one of her temples. Samantha was trying her best to get out of the hot seat.

Dr. Franzin moved back to the bed, checked

Samantha's pulse, and asked Rhonda to recheck her blood pressure and oxygen level. He went back to the folder and scribbled a few more notes before answering Samantha's question. "Your vitals are all good. Reflexes seem fine, but given your history of brain trauma, I think I'll order a scan just to be safe."

Before Samantha could protest, Dr. Franzin left the little room and returned to his desk to write out her orders. Samantha pulled the hair tie from her ponytail and shook loose her long brown hair. The long, wavy strands fell down her back and over one shoulder as she sighed.

"It's just one scan, and you'll be out of here in no time." Rhonda tried to assure her. "Besides, he's right. If your head hurt like you said it did, then it wouldn't be a bad idea to have it scanned."

"I know." Samantha huffed as she plopped back down on the bed, the table paper crinkling under her weight.

"So, how handsome was Mr. Deacon now that he wasn't knocking on death's door?" She gave a mischievous grin.

"Extremely." They laughed together but were interrupted again by the curtain sliding open.

"Laughter is the best medicine," Michael said to them as he walked over to Samantha and kissed her on the forehead. "Are you okay?" he asked her with worry in his eyes.

"I'm fine." Samantha nodded.

Her face turned from happy to something Rhonda couldn't discern. Michael slid his hand over Samantha's head and ran his fingers through her hair as he examined her face. It annoyed Rhonda how possessive Michael always seemed to be when they were together, but she knew better than to pry. She wondered how their relationship might change, before Michael interrupted her thoughts.

"What happened?" he asked as he sat on the edge of the exam table.

"I went for a run, and I guess I got too hot and passed out." Samantha shrugged as if it were something that happened all the time.

"You have to be more careful," he lectured. "You know I could set you up with one of my trainers, and you can use the gym any time you want. We have a doctor on staff, so he would be there any time." He was always trying to help Samantha and give her everything, Rhonda noticed, but Samantha never would accept anything extravagant from him. She was independent and wanted to make her own way. Rhonda admired her strength. It's not every day a girl gets in good with a rich and not to mention handsome guy like Michael McCray.

"Thank you, but you know I like to be outside rather than cooped up in a gym all day." She rubbed his arm and gave it an assuring squeeze.

"What do you say we get out of here and take a drive?" He got up from the bed, offering his hand to her.

"Actually," Rhonda interrupted. "Dr. Franzin has ordered some more tests, so she can't leave just yet."

Michael's face flashed with anger but quickly shifted into a polite smile. He held Samantha's hands in his and kissed the back of each. "The good doctor knows best. I'll get you later, then?"

"It's a date." Samantha's smile widened but didn't reach her eyes.

Rhonda kept her eyes trained on Michael as her

stomach tightened. He turned his head enough for her to see the tight set of his jaw as his face turned red. Her heart skipped a beat as she rubbed a hand over her chest.

When the emergency room doors closed behind him, she sat closer to Samantha. "What's his deal? Did you see his face?"

"I don't know. He's still mad about this morning. He's too overprotective sometimes, you know?"

"Definitely," Rhonda half-heartedly agreed. Her eyes were drawn to the closed doors he had left through. She couldn't shake the feeling that Michael could be the dangerous one.

Chapter 9

Michael stood like a statue outside of the emergency room doors as nurses and patients passed him in the hallway. He gritted his teeth and tightened his hands into fists as he tried to control his anger. He had hoped to have Samantha to himself this evening. Tonight was a crucial time for them. They were on a deadline, so he couldn't have anything, or anyone, get in his way. He breathed deep through his nose and let the air release slowly from his mouth.

He pulled a small phone from his inner jacket pocket and placed a call he had hoped he wouldn't have to make. After a couple of rings, a man with a deep and raspy voice answered.

"Yea," the voice spoke through the speaker.

"It's Michael. There's been a change in plans," he said as he smiled at an older couple that walked past him in the hallway.

"Where do you need us?" There was a hint of excitement in the raspy voice.

"She'll be discharged from Glenwood Memorial this evening. It should be dark by then, and knowing her, she'll walk home alone." He gave a quick description of Samantha to the hired goon. He disliked using men outside of his own team but didn't want to risk them being caught. "You can intercept her when the time's right."

"Piece of cake." The man snickered on the other end of the call.

Michael turned the corner and spotted a familiar face pushing an empty wheelchair in the direction he had just come from. He gritted his teeth with annoyance and watched Sebastion Walsh push through the emergency room doors with the wheelchair that was undoubtedly for Samantha.

"Take care of anyone that gets in your way." Michael snarled into the phone's tiny speaker. "Do I make myself clear?" Heat rose up his neck.

"Crystal," answered the man. "We know what to do." Men were laughing menacingly on the other end of the phone in the background.

"Good." Michael spoke in a grave tone. "I'd hate to find out you botched this task like your partners botched their last mission." He recalled the man's groveling before he pulled the trigger and ended his life after Deacon escaped from their facility. All the laughing ended abruptly on the other end of the call.

"Understood," said the man, and the call disconnected. He returned the phone to his pocket and disappeared through the automatic doors that led outside.

****

Deacon was driving his motorcycle through the back roads that snaked their way through and around Glenwood. Trees blurred as he sped past them. He was trying not to think about anything as the wheels of his bike churned up dust and rocks. The vibrations from his phone as it rang in the breast pocket of his leather jacket tingled his skin through the fabric. He wanted to ignore the call as the wind whipped through his hair, disheveling it.

He didn't want to stop his ride as it was one of the few things that helped his mood, but with everything at stake, he didn't want to risk it. He slowed the bike to a stop on the grassy shoulder of the forgotten road. He dropped the metal kickstand and let the bike rest as he answered the call.

"Where are you now?" Sebastion asked, his voice sounding tense.

"Just outside of town, near the Black Woods." Deacon dusted away as much dirt as he could from his jeans.

"What are you doing out there?" Sebastion asked. He already left his apartment and was heading back to the hospital. He hoped if he got there early enough, he could speak to Samantha before her shift ended, but he needed to talk to Deacon first. Sebastion was trying to use one hand to hold the cell phone and the other to steer his car through the tightly packed parking garage.

"Trying to clear my head." Sebastion heard Deacon say on the other end of the call. "What's up?"

Now that Sebastion had Deacon on the phone, he wasn't sure where to start. His mouth grew dry as he readied himself.

"Everything okay?" Deacon asked as he noticed Sebastion's hesitation. "Have you heard back from Oscar?"

"Yea, I did," Sebastion answered as he finally found an empty parking space.

"And?" Deacon asked. "Did he know anything?"

Sebastion parked the car and switched off the ignition before responding. "He did, actually," Sebastion said with hesitation. He just needed to be straightforward and ask. "How do you know Samantha?"

Deacon was silent for a long time before he answered his question. "We met a long time ago when we were children." He explained, slowly at first, and then it was like he was reminiscing. "The first time I ever saw her, she was unlike anyone I had ever met. She covered for me and saved me from being caught by some hunters. Her and her family, that is. She was eight then."

Sebastion waited and listened as Deacon continued.

"Her family knew about werewolves, so I didn't have to hide who I was when I was with her. She wasn't afraid of me. I felt normal with her. We grew up together and became close, but, well, you know the rest."

Sebastion's throat tightened from the sadness in Deacon's voice. "Oscar thinks Samantha is probably the one the hunters are after," he blurted out before he lost his nerve. His eyes crinkled as he chewed his lips, and he hoped he wouldn't have to repeat himself.

"What?" Deacon asked. "How does he know that?"

Sebastion sighed and got out of his car with his messenger bag in tow. He slammed his door shut and leaned hard against the green Honda Civic. "My dad sent him a letter explaining some research they found. It's why they were killed." Another car drove by him on its ascent to the higher levels of the garage. His skin chilled from the cool breeze it left as it passed.

When the car was out of sight, Sebastion continued. "Oscar said Samantha's parents' bodies were found around the same time as her accident. Kiren's pack killed them. There was no trace of her after that. I guess that's when she ended up here in Glenwood. She has amnesia, so I don't know how much she remembers." Sebastion paused to let the information soak in before he added with a sigh, "I'm sorry, man."

The phone was quiet for a long time until Deacon breathed into the speaker. It couldn't have been a coincidence that Kiren was involved. "We have to protect her." His stern voice made Sebastion's spine straighten as he walked.

The saying about not shooting the messenger popped into his mind as he shook his head. He hated being the messenger more than anything. This was not the conversation he wanted to have. "I'm at the hospital now." Sebastion headed to the elevator. "I'm going to try to talk to her, if she hasn't left yet."

"What are you going to say?" Deacon asked. "If she doesn't remember anything, you're going to freak her out."

"I'm working on it." Sebastion huffed. "It would help if you could talk to her too. She might remember you."

Deacon recalled the last twenty-four hours. "Maybe she already does."

"What do you mean?" Sebastion asked as the elevator made its descent to ground level. Sebastion always hated the tug on your stomach that an elevator gave you when it started to move. He held on to one of the rails that wrapped around the elevator walls. The lights were too bright, and the air was thick.

"She saved my life. It was after the run-in with those hunters at the factory. One of them shot me in the back when I was escaping. I don't know how I ended up at the bakery where she works, but there she was. She found me and got the bullet out in time."

"You forgot to mention that little nugget," Sebastion said, rolling his eyes.

"I woke up in her apartment."

Sebastion could almost hear a smile in his tone.

"It seemed like she recognized me at first, but I can't be sure. She was holding a baseball bat while she slept, so maybe not."

"Smart girl." Sebastion laughed. He didn't know Samantha Walker very well, but people only had good things to say about her. She was always smiling and helpful to everyone. He had never spoken to her before. He clenched his shaky hands into fists and took a few calming breaths. He could go through with this. He had to. "You didn't stay and talk to her?"

"No. I thought it would be safer if she weren't involved. I ran into her again earlier today at the hospital. I keep finding myself wherever she is."

Sebastion was quiet as he remembered part of the prophecy. "The second blood moon will bring forth a warrior, the first to be sacrificed."

"What?" Deacon asked.

Sebastion sighed and licked his dry lips as he connected the pieces. "You both have a role to play in this prophecy. I'll explain it all later. I'll get Samantha, and you need to get here. There is going to be a third blood moon tonight, and if Oscar's right, they're going to make a move on her." The elevator stopped and opened the doors that led out onto the carport that joined the side of the hospital.

"I'll be there." Deacon disconnected the call before he could say anything else.

****

Sebastion jogged into the hospital as his wet tennis shoes squeaked against the slick floor. His fingers fumbled with his badge until he managed to swipe the magnetic strip through the slit in the time clock. He was early for his shift but clocked in out of habit. He quickly put away his messenger bag and jacket into his locker in one of the employee lounges. As he left the lounge, he apologized as he collided with someone.

"Ah! Perfect timing, Mr. Walsh," said Dr. Franzin. He peered over his lowered glasses and passed him a slip of paper with his handwriting scrawled onto it. Sebastion was a certified nurse's aide here at the hospital and was one of Dr. Franzin's favorites, which usually made him feel important, but tonight, he just didn't have time to chat.

"I was just heading to—" Sebastion tried to say before he was cut off.

"I know it's been busy this evening, but one of our own needs us," Dr. Franzin said in his *we're a team* voice. He clapped his hand on his shoulder, giving it a light squeeze. "We have to take care of ourselves if we're going to take care of others, wouldn't you say?"

"Yes, sir, but—" Sebastion tried to say again.

"Miss Walker is in the ER, bed one," Dr. Franzin continued as he scribbled something down in a folder he was carrying.

Sebastion's eyes widened. "Who now?"

"Samantha Walker. She had a bit of an episode. I'd grab a wheelchair on the way. Just in case." And with that, Dr. Franzin walked off down the hallway and disappeared around the corner.

Sebastion stared at the corner that Dr. Franzin had slipped around before reading the order in his hand. The doctor's handwriting was always hard to decipher, but he grew familiar with it over the years. He wondered what happened to Samantha to need a scan of her head. *Am I too late?* His mouth became dry as he swallowed thick spit. Without another second of delay, he found the nearest wheelchair and headed to the emergency room.

Chapter 10

The emergency room's inner doors whooshed, and the screech of wheelchair wheels grew closer to Samantha. She peeked around the corner of the little room and noticed one of the hospital's aides pushing the wide chair in her direction. She recognized him as Sebastion Walsh. She had only seen him in passing, but any time his name was mentioned by a patient, it was always positive. Her coworkers spoke highly of him.

He was tall and wore black scrubs today. The deep contrast of the fabric against his flushed appearance was drastic. Samantha wondered if he was having a tough day. She blew air from her mouth to clear a loose curl that fell in her face. Here she was about to take more of his time for a scan she didn't need when he could be taking a break or helping someone who truly needed him. She pushed this thought aside and smiled at him as he locked the brakes on the old, tattered wheelchair.

"Your chariot has arrived," Rhonda said from her desk with a laugh. "Take good care of her, and don't let her talk you out of getting this scan."

Sebastion's brows raised after Rhonda said his name. He was quiet as his cheeks reddened, but he smiled sheepishly as he cast an awed glance over her. Her tan skin seemed darker against the light pink fabric of her scrubs. Her hair was in two long braids that lay across her shoulders. The corners of his lips twitched upward.

"I'll do my best," Sebastion said in a serious tone as if he truly meant it, and she didn't doubt that he did.

"Rough night, Sebastion?" Samantha asked from her place on the bed.

He faced her with another stunned expression. He rubbed the back of his neck as he struggled to keep eye contact with her now that they were inches apart.

"Nah," he replied as he moved to help her up from the bed and get her into the wheelchair. "I just clocked in. Dr. Franzin caught me in the hall."

"This isn't necessary. I'm okay, really." Samantha stood without taking his hand and eyed the wheelchair warily. "I could walk down to radiology. It's not far."

"Dr. Franzin's orders." Sebastion shrugged as he gestured to the chair with his outstretched arm. She gave in with a sigh and dropped down into the wide seat. As he turned the chair to leave the emergency room, Rhonda held the door open for them.

"Thank you." Sebastion smiled at Rhonda before he caught his foot on one of the chair's back wheels and stumbled. "Sorry," he said quickly. His cheeks burned a brighter shade of red.

Rhonda smiled back at him and gave Samantha's arm a light squeeze before she passed. "You're welcome and be careful. I'll catch up with you later. I'm almost done here."

"See you soon," Samantha said to her as Sebastion pushed through the hall.

It didn't take long for the radiologist to call her name and start the scan.

"I'll wait outside the door and help you back to the ER when you're finished." Sebastion helped her get out of the awkward chair.

She offered him a small smile and moved into the room. He really cared about his patients. "Thank you," she said before the radiologist closed the door behind her.

As she lay on the X-ray table, her mind wandered to Deacon and then to Michael. If she did get to talk to Deacon, she would find a way to introduce them, and hopefully, they would get along. The memory of Michael storming out of her apartment flashed through her mind. She suspected their meeting wouldn't go as well as she hoped, but only time would tell. She finally remembered someone from her past, but it wouldn't matter if everyone thought he was a bad guy.

Samantha thanked the radiologist and walked back out into the hallway where Sebastion stood next to the wheelchair, leaning against the opposite wall. The heavy click of the door closing behind her snapped him to attention. He reached for the wheelchair.

"I don't need the chair. I'm okay, I promise." She smiled at him reassuringly, and when he hesitated, she added, "I won't tell if you don't."

He parked the wheelchair by the entrance of the radiology department after folding it back together. "I'll walk you back at least."

"I should actually clock out. I'm still on the clock." A guilty feeling settled in her stomach.

"Oh yea," Sebastion said as she put a few steps between them. He ran his hand nervously through his hair. "I'm actually heading that way too."

"Oh. Okay." She gestured for him to take the lead as she fell into step with him. She counted tiles while they walked together.

They were silent the rest of the way until they reached the time clock which was a small electric box jutting out of the wall. It had been only a couple of hallways down from the hospital's radiology wing. She pulled her name badge from her pants pocket, and with a quick swipe, she slid it down the card slot which made a beeping noise as it registered her time punch.

"Are you hungry or thirsty?" Sebastion asked as she pocketed her name badge. "They're serving supper in the cafeteria right now. They make the best pesto chicken flatbread."

"That is one of my favorites, actually, and I'm starving."

"Great!" Sebastion exclaimed. "If we hurry, we might actually get a seat." He gestured in a gentlemanly way with his hands for Samantha to take the lead.

"Thank you, good sir." Samantha gave an exaggerated curtsy. Luckily, the cafeteria was on the same floor they were on. He held open the glass door that led them to a surprisingly short line leading to the buffet. After a few minutes, they each had trays of food. Samantha decided against dessert but grinned when Sebastion went for the lime-flavored gelatin snack. Once they had trays and drinks in hand, Sebastion paid for their meal, and the two of them moved to the less crowded area in the back where they found a small tan table with two chairs near the emergency exit door.

"The food smells delicious." Samantha grinned. "Thank you, Sebastion. I appreciate this. I'll pay you back."

"It's no trouble at all. Dig in."

They sat for a few minutes in silence as they ate their food and drank their sodas through bendy straws from foam cups. Sebastion was nervously shaking his leg, and he hadn't touched his food while hers was almost gone. He chewed on his inner jaw as if something was on his mind.

"You don't have to babysit me. I'm one hundred percent okay. You have other patients to get to, I'm sure. I'll just head home and get some rest. Thank you again for the food."

"You're welcome, and it's no trouble, really. I clocked in early this evening, so I have some time until I have to officially report in. I could drive you home?"

Sebastion's cinnamon eyes and his boy-next-door face was sweet and caring, but Samantha couldn't take up any more of his time. "It's fine, really. You've done more than enough."

"It's no trouble. I insist. I'll take care of this and will be right back." He gathered up everything on their table so fast he almost spilled one of the drinks.

He caught the cup before it spilled more than a single drop. He worked his way slowly through the crowded cafeteria to the trash bins at the far side of the room. While he was waiting in another line, Samantha slipped out of the emergency door exit and rushed down the stairs. Normally, she wouldn't act this way, but she was anxious to get outside and back to her apartment. She enjoyed being a nurse and helping people, but she hated being a patient herself.

The cool night air washed over her as she pushed through the heavy door that opened to the back of the hospital. Samantha loved autumn weather, but it always took her a few weeks to get used to the shorter days. The picnic tables were empty at this time, and the area was quieter than the busy cafeteria. She jogged around the back lot so she wouldn't be noticed if Sebastion was following her. A pang of guilt tugged at her for leaving him the way she did, but hopefully she could make up for it later. Sebastion was a nice guy, and he meant well, but she needed time alone to think.

She was behind one of the supply buildings before she chanced a quick peek over her shoulder to see if she was being followed, but there was no one there. She leaned against the rough siding of the building. With a deep breath, she turned her eyes up to the sky and was basked in the blood moon's bright red light. She smiled up at it as a cool breeze blew through her hair. She didn't mind the chill as she admired the view. The sky was dark with clouds, so only a few of the brightest stars peaked through. The moon was bright and full as its force pulled at the night owl in her.

The light breeze turned stronger as a streak of lightning lit up her surroundings, followed by thunder that rumbled in her chest. The rain formed a gray sheet in the distance, and she knew it was heading in her direction.

"Great," she said aloud. She thought about returning to the hospital and taking Sebastion up on his offer to drive her home but decided against it. She would have to explain why she ran out on him if she went back. She glanced over her shoulder one last time then made her decision. She didn't live far away from the hospital, so she would be there in no time. *A little rain never killed anyone.* The first few drops of rain hit her hair and splashed on the tip of her nose.

She pushed herself off the wall and shook the soreness from her legs. If she cut through the loading area that connected to the supply buildings, she could cut the distance in half to her building. The wind pushed the rain all around her as she hurried to the loading bay. She was soaked already and was kicking herself for not just going back inside the hospital. It was her stubbornness that wouldn't allow her to accept help.

Before Samantha could self-reflect any more, she heard an aluminum can bounce across the asphalt as if someone kicked it. She stopped and turned toward the sound but didn't see anyone. She broke out in a sweat as fear crept its way into her gut. She turned back to the path. Lightning brightened the area, showing a man as he walked out from the shadows.

"Where are you off to in such a hurry?" the man asked her in a raspy voice. The tip of his cigarette glowed bright red as he inhaled deeply. His dark eyes roamed over her. She could tell he was taller and bigger than her as he moved closer. She had to stay calm.

"Just waiting for my boyfriend to get here," Samantha lied as she willed her voice not to waver. "He's supposed to pick me up. He'll be here any second." She backed away from him, putting as much distance between them as possible.

"I don't think so." She heard the man say as he dropped the cigarette to the ground, snuffing it out with the toe of his heavy boot. Water dripped from the bill of his cap as he kicked the can before returning his dark gaze back to her. "No one's coming for you tonight." He paused long enough to flash another menacing grin. "Except for us, that is." As he spoke, he gestured with one hand in the direction behind her.

The wind was cold on her wet skin, and the rain stung her eyes. Her pulse pumped in her ears, causing her breathing to pick up as she slowly turned around. She forced her eyes up from the ground just in time to see two men closing in on her. The man to her left was tall and slender. His long coat was slick from the rain. The man to her right was like a giant. He wore a dingy white sleeveless shirt that fit him tightly across his hulking form. He wore black pants inside of heavy work boots that splashed water with every stomp toward her. He was smiling as he got closer.

Samantha backed up cautiously, trying to keep all three men in her sights as she thought of what to do. There was no one to help her. The streets were empty. "If you get any closer, I'll scream," she said to the men as she held up her hands in a stay back gesture.

"Please do," said the giant with a smirk. His eyes darkened. "There's no one here but us, sweetheart." The man spoke with an accent she couldn't place. Lightning and thunder crashed simultaneously, causing her to jump.

She regarded each of them and knew she needed to act fast. She ran as hard and as fast as she could toward an opening that led to the street. She prayed that she'd make it before they caught up to her. She was coming up on the sidewalk when another man stepped out in front of her. She tried to stop, but the ground was slick with rain causing her feet to slide out from under her. She hit hard and groaned as a numbing pain bloomed on her hip. The asphalt scraped her palms when she tried to catch herself.

The man in front of her also wore all-black clothes covered by a dripping wet raincoat. His long blond hair was pulled back in a low ponytail. A few loose strands of hair swayed as he moved toward her, bending at the waist to grab her, but she kicked him hard under his chin.

The man cursed and covered his mouth with his hands. She tried to pull herself up from the ground when she realized someone was behind her. The giant was faster than she thought as he hauled her up from the ground and twisted his hand in her long hair.

She straightened up as fast as she could and bashed the giant's nose with the back of her head. His skull was as hard as a brick wall when she hit him. Stars erupted in front of her eyes, but she shook them away as he let go of her hair and staggered backward. She was about to run again when the other men grabbed each of her arms and slammed her against the wall to which she was closest. She struggled with them, but their grip was too tight.

"Let me go! Help!" Her screams were drowned out by thunder. She breathed heavily and tried to think how she was going to get out of this.

"Hurry up!" the man with the cap said to the giant. Her face was turned in his direction as one of them pushed her cheek against the rough cement. She gritted her teeth as the jagged surface tore into her flesh.

"My pleasure," the man said with a sniff of his bleeding nose. He pulled out a large syringe from a bag she hadn't noticed before. She struggled hard against them, but they held fast to her arms and pushed her hard against the building.

"Don't do this!" She pleaded as the moonlight glinted off the tip of the syringe. The large needle punctured the crease of her elbow as she struggled to get free. It moved around under her skin, causing her stomach to grow sick. She forced herself to stay conscious. All she could do was wait for the sting from whatever they were about to inject her with, but the sensation never came. Her blood filled the syringe. She watched as it bubbled and steamed up the clear tube.

Wooziness swam through her as thunder rumbled in the distance, but this time, it sounded different. She blinked to clear the rain from her eyes as she continued to struggle.

"What was that?" the man with the ponytail asked the others as he whipped his head around to scan the area, sending more water into her eyes. Samantha thought it was fear on his face then.

"Just thunder," said the other man that was now gripping Samantha's arm so tight she thought he was going to crush the bone within. "Hurry up!" he shouted to the giant. The needle withdrew from her arm as warm blood mixed with the rain on her skin.

"We got what we need," he said with a grin. His blood was running down onto his teeth as he spoke.

"Let's take her back to the van." The man with the cap lifted his face up to the dark sky. "I hate all this rain, and just in case that's not enough, they'll have more on tap," he said with a shake of his head.

The man to her right let her arm go and grabbed a handful of her hair, jerking her away from the wall. That strange thunder rumbled again, but the more she listened, she realized it wasn't thunder. It was a motorcycle. The men heard it too as they pulled together and snarled in the direction of the sound. The silence was broken by a deep, wild growl echoing through the shadows. They all turned to see two glowing eyes peering out at them like the eyes of a wolf, but they were at the height of a man.

Her vision grew blurry as she strained to see clearly. She blinked furiously when another streak of lightning lit up the shadows, revealing Deacon as he bared his teeth. He was soaking wet, his shirt clinging to his body, showing every chiseled feature of his muscles. His eyes were narrowed as each breath blew through the rain that slid down his tightened face. There was something different about him, but the shadows covered him in darkness before she could discern the change. The man that gripped her hair pulled her in front of him and wrapped his arm tightly around her throat. She brought her hands up to pull against the force of the man's arm that was cutting off her air supply.

She managed to move his arm enough for her to try biting through the sleeve of his jacket. This only angered him, causing him to pull harder at her hair. He moved his arm enough for her to hit him hard in the ribs with her elbow. He let go of her hair, and she spun around to face him. With all the strength she could muster, she punched him hard in the face. On contact, her fist exploded with pain, and blood spurted from his nose.

"You broke my nose!" the man cursed at her through the blood gurgling down his throat.

Samantha held her aching wrist close to her chest. Before she moved, a large hand latched on her shoulder. It was the giant. He was glaring down at her. He swung his other hand at her, landing a hit across her face. The force knocked her to the ground, splashing water up around her. The man kicked her hard in the stomach and ribs. She tried to roll away from him, but he continued to kick her in the back until they heard a man scream.

She could barely move but forced herself to raise her head. At that moment, two men sailed through the air one after the other. They hit the ground hard and didn't move. Her stomach lurched at the sound of breaking bones. The giant grabbed her by the back of her neck and wrenched her to her feet. Her body ached as he pulled her in front of him like a shield. She was having a tough time breathing, but she managed to stay on her feet.

"Let. Her. Go," a voice growled in front of them. A blurry image of Deacon appeared in front of her. Something was different about him. His features were more animal, and his eyes were glowing a bright blue. Drops of rain slid down his arms and dripped from sharp claws. As his breath fogged up the air around him, she could have sworn she saw fangs. She had to be seeing things after everything that had happened.

The giant laughed deeply in her ear. It gave her chills and made the hair on her arms stand up.

"Can't do, mate," he snapped. "I have my orders. Besides—" He paused to smell Samantha's hair and neck. "—a thing like you wouldn't know what to do with something this sweet," he said with a dark grin. His ugly face was clear to see under the yellow glow of the streetlamp. He had a long scar that ran down through one of his eyes. He smelled of diesel and sweat. The scent brought bile up from her stomach that she tried to push down.

She wanted to pass out as she struggled with the giant's hand in her hair, but he only tightened his grip. Deacon's roar startled her. The sound resonating in her chest. The next moments seemed to happen in slow motion. The giant moved and threw her to the ground. There was the sound of a gun exploding, and the last thing she saw before the darkness came over her was the glint of moonlight reflecting off the smooth surface of something metal. Pain exploded as her head connected with it, and she blacked out.

Chapter 11

The piercing screech of tires dragged Samantha out
of the darkness. As she slowly opened her eyes, her ears
rang, and her vision was blurred. She blinked slowly to
relieve the stinging as she was bounced in her seat. Wind
whipped loose strands of her hair around her face and
stole her breath away. She brought a shaky hand to her
forehead where her fingers met a warm and sticky liquid
flowing down the side of her face. Fear set in, causing
her to shift in her seat, but a strong arm tightened around
her, holding her steady.

"Where are we going?" she asked in a weak voice.
She focused on her breathing as her head spun.

"Somewhere safe." A comforting voice spoke into
her ear. She gave into the warmth that was coming off
his body despite the frigid wind and rain as she slipped
back into the darkness.

A falling sensation gripped Samantha, but before
she could slam into the ground, her body jerked her
awake. Her head throbbed despite the soft pillow she
now rested on. The deep brown lofted ceiling above her
was very different from the flat ceiling of her apartment.
She didn't recognize this place. The bright lights stung
her eyes. Afraid to move too quickly, she slid her hands
along the smooth sheet under her body and brought them
up to inspect her head. Instead of the warm, slick feel of
her blood, her fingers moved across the soft, smooth

surfaces of gauze and tape. She winced at how tender the wound was.

With her movement came a familiar scent. It was warm and masculine, and it filled every inch of her senses. A heavy comforter was pulled up to just below her waist. She was no longer in her scrub uniform but was wearing a long T-shirt that didn't belong to her. It barely covered her, and there was nothing underneath. This jolted her out of her coziness and back to the reality of what happened.

She slung the comforter aside and jumped out of the bed. A sharp pain twisted in her head, which sent a wave of nausea through her. The room was spinning, and she was shaking. Her body was sore, and her legs were unable to hold her weight as she reached out to steady herself on the edge of the large bed. Before she could tumble to the hardwood floor, someone caught her with strong arms.

The scent of mint and leather filled her. She angled her head to see cool eyes that brightened as he held her close to his chest. In those eyes gleamed concern along with something else. "Where are you going in such a hurry?" he said as he held her in his arms. "You looked like you were comfortable." A crooked grin replaced his worried expression.

"Where am I? Why did you bring me here?" She tried to clear the fog from her mind.

"You're safe. This is my house." He sat her down gently on the edge of the mattress.

As she took in her surroundings, she realized she was in a small cabin. The space was open, allowing her to see the living room and small kitchen. A door to the far right must have led to the bathroom. The space was small but cozy. The dark hardwood floors contrasted against tan walls with white borders. The ceiling rose high above them. There was a single nightstand and a tall dresser at the foot of the bed. She caught a glimpse of herself in the round mirror that sat on top of the dresser's smooth wood surface.

Her breath caught in her throat as she surveyed the damage. Her lip was swollen in one corner and already starting to bruise. A small patch of crimson had soaked to the surface of the gauze on her forehead. Her hair twisted and curled over her shoulders and down her back in knots. She was a mess.

"Why'd you bring me here?" she demanded.

"To return the favor." Deacon shrugged his shoulders.

Chills ran down her body, drawing her attention to just how short the T-shirt she was wearing really was. It barely covered her thighs as her long legs were propped over the bed's edge. She pulled at the shirt hem, willing the fabric to grow a few more inches. Blood flushed her tight and swollen cheeks. The night's events ran through her mind as she focused on the grainy lines in the hardwood flooring.

"Those men…Who were they, and why did they want my blood?" She couldn't meet his eyes as she spoke.

He removed a white throw from the bed's headboard and covered her legs. The fabric scraped across the raised edges of the peeling tape. He didn't respond to her questions. Instead, he stared through the window behind the bed. His brow was pinched together in the middle, and his eyes grew distant. His chiseled jaw ticked as he bowed his head.

"Deacon?" she said his name in a faint voice. She hoped she really had remembered him before and that she wasn't losing her mind and making a complete fool of herself. He trained his cool blue eyes on her face. The corners of his lips ticked upward before he ran his hand over his mouth.

"What do you remember? From before all this?" He eyed her cautiously as if saying the wrong thing would send her screaming for the hills.

"Not much," Samantha admitted, "but things are starting to come back. I remembered us when we were children. We were playing in a playground somewhere. I'm not sure where. That's when I remembered your name. That is your name, right?" Her eyes shone with tears that threatened to fall as she recalled the memory. "Why didn't you stay back at my apartment, and why did you run from me outside the hospital?"

"That's my name. I didn't want to get you involved, but you already were." Deacon squeezed her hand that now held his.

"Involved in what?" He was avoiding her question. She stood up from the bed again, ignoring the aches and pains. She stood in front of him and softly turned his head so that he was facing her. He was even more handsome now that she was standing this close to him. His thick, brown hair was tousled in a styled way. His light blue eyes pierced into her soul. The color made his long eyelashes darker. As she held his face, the stubble of his five-o'clock shadow scraped her palm. He was beautiful.

Another memory formed in her eyes. Her head throbbed as flashes from her past came forward. The memories came and went like she was fanning through pages of a picture book. She saw faces she didn't have names for, and so many emotions hit her at once. She gasped and put her head in her hands. The strength of her legs failed her, but Deacon slid his strong arms around her waist. She clasped her hands behind his neck as he picked her up and laid her back down on the bed in one swift motion. He covered her with the comforter and pushed back the hair that hung over her face.

He stared at her as if she was the most beautiful woman he'd ever seen. Anger and sadness filled his eyes as he regarded her injuries. He sat down on the bed next to her and wiped away a tear that had fallen onto her cheek. "I'm sorry."

"For what?" she asked him as she turned her hazel eyes toward him. He traced his index finger around the black-and-white pattern on his comforter as if he couldn't face her. "For leaving all those years ago?"

His eyes snapped to hers in surprise. He nodded and swallowed hard as if he was afraid to speak at that moment. His chest rose as he breathed deeply.

"It's okay." Samantha's voice broke. "You're here now." She smiled at him. Another tear rolled down her cheek.

"How do you feel?"

"I'll be okay." She picked at the bandages on her hands. "How do you feel?" she asked him, still not sure how he was able to fight four men in his condition.

"I'm fine. Why do you ask?"

"You shouldn't be up running around and fighting with a gunshot wound. You were in bad shape. I was worried about you." She sat up in the bed.

His face fell. "You don't remember everything."

"Then tell me. Please. I want to remember. I need

to." She clasped her hands over his forearms and ducked her head to meet his eyes.

"The only way to tell you is to show you." He stood up from the bed, and in one fluid motion, he pulled his black shirt up and off over his head. She was stunned at first by his actions, but she couldn't help but admire his toned body once again. His strong abs and muscles rippled from his movement, but what Samantha didn't see was a single scratch or scar.

She met his gaze. He remained quiet as he turned around to show her his back. Samantha got on her knees and moved closer to him so she could examine his tightly muscled back. In the place where she had dug out the bullet was only smooth skin. There wasn't even a scar.

"How can this be?" She slid a shaking finger over his shoulder blade.

Without turning to face her, Deacon explained. "People like me, they can heal faster than humans."

"People like you?" Samantha explored his back for any sign of a scar, but there was nothing. His skin was flawless.

"Do you trust me?" he asked.

Samantha pulled her aching hand to her chest with hesitation. "I do," she finally said.

He slowly turned to face her. Her heart slammed in her chest with anxious anticipation.

She breathed in a quick breath that brought a stabbing pain to her ribs. He kept his head down, but his features had changed. His hands were longer, and there were sharp claws where human fingernails had once been. She drew a line with her eyes up his strong arms and over his chest. She slid her hand along the rough stubble on his chin and lifted his face to hers. His ears had grown to a point, and his brow seemed to become more animalistic. Even his hair had grown slightly longer. His brow was more pronounced and gave him a menacing appearance. His soft lips parted slightly, revealing long sharp teeth beneath.

He was a beast, but his eyes stayed the same as he opened them to meet her gaze. A sharp pain threatened to crack her skull, forcing her to sit as she moved a hand to her forehead. More images flashed through her mind. The sight of him was the key that unlocked the box that held her memories.

"Are you okay?" Deacon asked her. He kept still as if he was afraid to move or to try to touch her. Her chest heaved as heat flooded her face and neck.

She removed her hand from her eyes and smiled at him as tears flowed freely from her eyes. With a sob, she threw her arms around his neck and squeezed him as tight as she could. "I remember," she said through tears. "I remember."

His werewolf form faded away, and he gently put his arms around her waist as she sobbed into his shoulder. Her tears slipped over his skin as he tightened his grip around her. "I never thought I would see you again, and to be with you now and holding you...I can't believe it."

She hoped this wasn't all a dream she would soon be waking up from. He held her and rubbed her back until the crying stopped and she found the strength to pull away.

"You should get some rest," he said to her in a deep voice as he tucked a strand of hair behind her ear.

She nodded and wiped away her fallen tears. Exhaustion was setting in, and her mind was spinning with thoughts. His hand slid against her leg as he helped her back under the covers. She caught his hand before he could leave her side.

"Stay with me?" she asked in a small voice.

He ran his free hand down the back of his head and rubbed his neck. He clenched and unclenched his fist as it dropped to his side.

"Just until I fall asleep." The feel of his thumb moving against her hand calmed her.

He nodded and walked to the other side of the bed. He lay down next to her and slid cautiously toward her. Even though the room was warm, and she was covered by the heavy comforter, she was shaking. His body heat radiated next to her, but he didn't touch her. There was a wound on every inch of her body from the fight she put up with the hunters, but she needed the comfort of him against her.

She inched closer to him and nuzzled her head into his shoulder. She breathed in his musky scent of mint and leather that filled the space between them. She crossed her arms over her chest and let the heat from his body warm her. His body remained rigid.

"You can relax," she said to him. "I won't break."

He tucked her hair behind her ear and trailed his fingers along the edge of her chin.

"Ah!" She winced as she turned over. Her breath caught in her throat, causing him to lean away. "I'm sorry." Her ribs may not be broken, but they were very sore.

"Don't be sorry," he whispered in her ear as he moved closer and put a protective arm gently over her side. "Just get some rest." He brushed her hair off her shoulder, revealing the smooth curve of her neck. She clasped his hand, pulling it to her face. She kissed it softly and held his arm tightly to her chest.

"Thank you. For being there." He held tight to her hand and gently kissed the top of her head. The glow from his eyes shone in the dim lighting of the room. He could keep her safe, no matter what they faced. Her muscles relaxed, and her breathing became even with sleep. Nothing was going to separate them again.

****

Waking up to Deacon was one of the greatest sights Samantha had ever seen. He was more than handsome. His sleeping face was serene. It was different this time compared to the night she had saved his life. Then, his features were tense with pain and seemed tortured, but now as the sun shone over him, he was at peace.

"You know, it's rude to stare." He spoke with his eyes still closed.

Her face burned red-hot, and like she was a little girl again, she covered her face with the blanket to hide her embarrassment.

Deacon pulled the blanket slowly away. He was grinning at her now, and the sight of his smile brought butterflies to her stomach. The two watched each other until he broke the silence.

"Feeling better?" he asked, still grinning.

"A little." She nodded and smiled back.

"Good." His grin spread wide across his face, showing perfect white teeth. He cleared some of the flyaways from her face as he fought the urge to laugh.

"What?" She covered her mouth with her hand and hoped she didn't have dry drool on her face.

"Your hair's a disaster." His laugh was warm and wonderful, and it wrapped around her heart, soothing the tiniest fractures. She couldn't remember every detail from her past, but everything was starting to come back to her. She hoped she would remember his face as it was now and how his laugh made her feel in that moment.

His face turned serious. He was still lying next to her in his bed, but his mind was far away. He slowly returned his focus back to her eyes as he spoke.

"I searched for you," he said softly. "When I got to your parents' house, the doors were open, and it looked like everyone left in a hurry. I searched for weeks, but it was as if you never existed."

She held his gaze as he tucked a loose strand of her bangs behind one ear and worked his strong fingers through her hair. She held his warm hand to her cheek before he could pull away, and nuzzled into his palm. His touch was everything she ever needed. A tear slid down her cheek and into his palm when she closed her eyes. All the emotions she was feeling were building within herself, begging to be released before she exploded.

She opened her eyes and slowly met his gaze. Her breath quickened as he stared at her intently. Without thinking, she pressed her lips against his. They were warm and soft against her split lip, but she ignored the pain. He held her face in his hands as their kiss deepened. She wanted to wrap her legs around his hard body and kiss him endlessly.

She pressed herself onto him as heat shot through her middle. Her body craved every smooth stroke of his fingers against her skin. Was this happening because of everything they'd been through, or is this something they were allowed to have? With his hands holding her body tightly against his, he wanted her just as much as she wanted him. She wanted to kiss every inch of him.

The front door clanged against the wall as it was thrown open, a familiar voice filling the room.

"Deacon, I saw your bike outside!" called Sebastion as he kicked the door shut with his foot. He was carrying a bag of groceries that blocked his view until he sat it down. "Why didn't you answer your phone when— Oh! Dear! God!" Sebastion exclaimed as he spotted them together. He quickly turned his back to them and covered his eyes with one hand.

With their kiss interrupted, Deacon hopped out of the bed and walked toward the living room area where Sebastion stood. He glanced back at Samantha with an odd expression on his face. She sat up straight against the headboard of the bed and pulled the cover up to her shoulders.

"Well, I see you found Samantha." Sebastion continued to cover his eyes. "Don't mind me." He moved closer to the front door. "I'm just going to leave now." He smashed into the wall next to the front door and groaned as he rubbed his nose.

"It's okay, Sebastion," Deacon said. "Nothing happened. Don't you knock?"

"Well, I didn't expect you to be, you know, involved?" Sebastion said, gesturing toward the bed. His eyes fell on her bandages and bruised face. "What happened?"

"The hunters got to her before I could." Deacon walked back toward the bed. He picked his shirt off the floor and pulled it over his head. Sebastion followed him.

"I'm so sorry." His mouth opened and closed as if he didn't know what to say.

"You two know each other?" Samantha asked, feeling very awkward in nothing but a T-shirt as she held on to the blanket like a life vest.

"Oh yea," Sebastion said. "We go way back." He scratched the back of his neck with a rough hand. His tone came out sarcastic and harsh. His eyes were red, and his movements were jittery.

"Sebastion," Deacon said in a warning tone.

"I'm sorry." Sebastion sighed as he took a seat at the foot of the bed, but he quickly jumped back up. "Oh, God...Sorry." His face turned red. "Wait..." Sebastion stood back and recalled what he saw when he first walked into Deacon's house. A silly grin spread across Sebastion's face as he crossed his arms and faced Deacon. "You..." he said in a joking manner. "I like it. You two make a good couple."

Deacon shook his head at Sebastion and ushered him out of the house.

"What?" Sebastion said, laughing now. "I do. Ya, know? If the situation was better." Sebastion continued to babble as Deacon pushed him outside.

"We'll talk in a minute," Deacon coaxed as he closed the door behind him.

"It's a normal thing!" Sebastion shouted through the closed door. "It may even be good for you!" he yelled as he walked off the porch and onto the yard as he continued to talk more to himself than to Deacon. "If she wasn't destined to be the end of werewolves everywhere, that is." Sebastion's mood turned sour as he realized that Deacon more than likely heard that last part. As soon as he said it, he regretted it, but he guessed that didn't matter. *It is what it is.* The cat was out of the bag, and they were nowhere near a solution to their problem.

"I'm sorry," Sebastion said, hoping Deacon was still listening. He found himself apologizing a lot lately and for things he didn't do. If all this turned out well, it'd be a miracle, and a miracle was what they needed more than anything. Sebastion walked back to his car and dropped hard into the driver's seat.

Chapter 12

Deacon leaned his back on the door. He did hear what Sebastion said, but an apology wasn't necessary. Deacon understood their situation and couldn't allow himself to let down his guard. Being with Samantha like this wasn't smart. Love made you weak, and they couldn't afford that right now. Their lives depended on him.

"Sebastion knows about all this?" Samantha got up from the bed. She had the blanket pulled around her as she walked toward him. "About hunters and werewolves?"

"It's a long story." She walked toward him with a hint of concern on her face. His shirt rode up her long legs with each step she took. His mouth went dry as her intoxicating scent continued to fill the house. He couldn't let his thoughts dwell on how right it was to have her here. "It's a story that isn't completely mine to tell." His eyes were set firm as he held his breath.

Samantha nodded as if deciding not to press the matter any further. Her thoughts wandered back on the kiss they shared. "Deacon—"

"It's okay," he interrupted. The two locked eyes and held each other's gaze until she broke the silence.

"I should go." She turned away from him and padded around the room, searching. "Can you take me to my apartment? I need to get some clothes and let Rhonda know I'm okay. I was supposed to go back to see her. I've not been gone that long." She raised an eyebrow at him, waiting for his response. He chewed his lip and brought one hand up to scratch the back of his neck. "What is it?"

"It's been three days since you left the hospital," he admitted.

"I've been here for three days?!" She gasped as panic slipped into her voice. "That's three days of work missed. Unexcused!" She dropped the cover to the floor and paced, her voice climbing an octave. "I'm fired. I'm so fired, and Rhonda…Oh! She's going to kill me!" she continued. "She'll have the National Guard out looking for me."

Deacon took her arms and pulled her to him. Her mood affected him in a way he didn't understand. "It will be okay," he assured her. "Call her." He gestured to his phone on the nightstand. "Let her know you're safe, and you can use the bathroom to clean up. We'll get your clothes." Deacon gave her an assuring smile and headed for the door.

"But I don't have my keys," Samantha stammered. "They're in my locker at work."

He faced her before he left the cabin, and with a sly grin, he said, "I don't need keys." Then he left, closing the door behind him.

Once outside, Deacon found his porch empty. He found Sebastion sitting in his car. He walked over to where he was parked on the dirt road that led to his place. Without speaking to him, Deacon pulled the passenger door open and got in the vehicle. The vanilla-scented pine tree swung from the rearview mirror. Sebastion gave him a sideways glance but remained silent.

"The hunters jumped her when she left the hospital." Deacon peered at his house through the Civic's windshield. "I barely got there in time. I took her from them, but one of them got away with her blood. She was hurt, and I didn't know what else to do, so I brought her here." His fists clenched and unclenched at his sides as the memory came back to him. He didn't want to think about what might've happened if he got there too late.

"Well, that's just crappy. What's the plan now?"

"She needs some supplies from her apartment," Deacon said. "She's going to let someone named Rhonda know she's okay. Do you know her?"

"Who?" Sebastion asked. "Rhonda? Yea. She works at the hospital. Her and Samantha are close."

"Will she tell her everything that's going on?" Deacon asked.

"Probably." Sebastion rubbed his forehead. "I don't know."

Deacon rubbed his mouth in contemplation.

"Look, man. I tried to tell her what was going on, but I couldn't find the words. I was afraid I would freak her out and she'd run off." Sebastion licked his dry lips.

"I guess she ran off anyway." Deacon laid his head against the headrest.

"Yep." Sebastion blew air through his nose. "That she did."

"I'm starting to feel like we don't have any control in this." Deacon's eyes wandered over the forest that surrounded his house. "I keep ending up everywhere that she is, but I don't think it's a good thing. I have this feeling that someone's going to die."

"We can't think like that. We can't let them win." Sebastion was glaring down at the black steering wheel of his car, fiddling with a loose piece of plastic from the steering wheel cover.

Deacon thought about this as they drove into town and toward Samantha's apartment. Different buildings that lined the streets of Glenwood drifted by them. He never thought a small city like this would hold so much. When he first bought his cabin here, he never imagined Samantha would be so close, but now he believed it was more than just a coincidence. They were meant to be brought together, but for what he wasn't sure.

"Which one is her place?" Sebastion asked as they neared the residential area of town.

"On down this street and on the right." Deacon pointed the building out to him.

Sebastion angled his car into one of the parking lots. The two got out and surveyed the area for any sign of someone being set up for surveillance. Once it was safe to go in, they made their way up to the building, glancing over their shoulders as they went.

"What's her apartment number?" Sebastion asked.

"I don't know for sure," Deacon replied. "I have an idea."

Sebastion blew out air and took in the empty hallway. They were lucky to get buzzed in by someone who must be a little too trusting in the building. His anxiety grew the longer they were out in the open.

Deacon closed his eyes and focused on Samantha's scent. He knew they were on the right floor, since he had taken the fire escape down last time he was here.

"I've got it." They walked by several doors. Each one released a different fragrance. A spicy chili scent burned his nose before he stopped. Deacon wrapped his palm around the brass doorknob and was about to break in when he froze.

"What is it?" Sebastion asked as he took in Deacon's concerned expression.

"There's someone inside," he warned.

Deacon turned the knob slowly and noticed it was already unlocked. He pressed his index finger against his lips, signaling Sebastion to be quiet. The door moaned as it creaked open. The room was dim compared to the bright hallway lights. The sun was streaming through the sheer curtains in the living room. As they slowly entered the foyer, Deacon listened for any sign of the intruder's location.

As they moved past the kitchen, they jumped when a scream pierced the silence. They turned to their left just in time to see a woman as she swung a baseball bat at them. Deacon pushed Sebastion out of the way and barely avoided her attack himself. She lunged at them again with the bat, and it connected with a wall behind them, cracking it. Deacon grabbed the bat from her and threw it to the ground as drywall crumbled to the floor.

"What the hell are you doing in here?" The woman shot into the kitchen and grabbed a butcher knife from a knife block that sat on the counter. "If you even try to touch me right now, believe me, you will pull back a nub. I'm not playin'." She had the knife pointed at Deacon's chest when the kitchen light flickered on.

"Rhonda?" Sebastion's heart banged in his chest.

"Sebastion!?" she yelled. "What the hell are you doin' here? Are you crazy? I could've killed you."

"I can see that," Sebastion said from behind Deacon as he eyed the large knife she was still holding. "Do you care to put that down?"

Rhonda dropped her eyes down at the weapon in her

hands but tightened her grip on the black handle. "Not until you explain to me why you're in Samantha's apartment?"

"We could ask you the same thing," Deacon said to her. He still had his hands up in surrender.

"You're that guy," Rhonda said. "Deacon or whatever. Where's Samantha?" she asked him as she raised the knife back to his chest.

"She's safe. We can take you to her if you want, or you can call her?" Deacon spoke without taking his eyes off Rhonda. "Sebastion, call my phone."

Sebastion pulled out his phone and tapped the screen. He put it on speakerphone before sliding it across the counter to her.

After a few rings, Samantha's voice echoed in the kitchen. "Um, hello?"

"Samantha!" Rhonda said. "Thank God! Are you okay? Where have you been?!"

"Rhonda?" Samantha's voice cracked through the phone. "Are you with Sebastion?"

"Yea." She eyed the two men. "We're in your apartment. I've been worried sick about you. When you didn't come back to the hospital, I thought you went home, but I couldn't reach you. I called the cops, but a lot of good they did me." Rhonda rolled her eyes.

"I'm sorry. I'm okay though, I promise. Deacon and Sebastion are there to bring me some clothes. Will you help them find everything?"

"Clothes?" Rhonda asked incredulously. She raised her brows at Deacon. "Uh huh," she said to the room. "I see."

"It's not like that," Samantha assured her. "I'll explain everything when you get here."

"Okay, but just so you know, you're givin' me ulcers. I thought you should know that."

Samantha laughed and apologized again. "I'll see you soon." Samantha ended the call, and Rhonda faced Deacon and Sebastion. She was still pointing the knife at them. All three of them eyed its sharp tip as she slipped it back into its place in the knife block.

"Don't make me regret this," Rhonda hissed as she walked into Samantha's bedroom.

Deacon and Sebastion sighed with relief. "So that's Rhonda?"

"That'd be her." Sebastion smirked.

Deacon only raised his eyebrows and nodded.

Chapter 13

Samantha disconnected the call and returned Deacon's cell phone back to the nightstand. She had just got out of the shower when she heard the phone ring, so now, she was standing in only a towel. Luckily, she managed to find a pair of sweatpants and another long T-shirt that was big on her, but it would work until they got back with her clothes. Rhonda was going to be mad, but she hoped everything would be okay soon.

Samantha slipped into the warm clothes. The soft and comfortable fabric slid against her scraped and bruised body. She still couldn't believe she had slept in Deacon's bed for three days, but there was nothing she could do about that now. She had a concussion from her fight with the hunters. Everything that had happened lately was wearing her down. She wasn't back to her normal self, but she was improving.

She ran her fingers through her tangled hair and managed to find her shoes by the front door. Everything in the house was organized and clean. It wasn't how she thought a bachelor werewolf would keep his area, but she liked it. Samantha opened the front door and peeked out.

As she walked out onto the porch, she noticed two wood chairs with a small table in between them. The steps of the porch led off to a walking path that connected to the dirt road that Samantha assumed connected to one of the main roads that led back into town. She took a walk around the property to get a little sun and fresh air. She admired the small backyard that was lined with trees that led deep into the Black Woods.

A lot of the trees were still full of life, but scattered throughout were the gnarled and twisted branches of trees that had already lost their leaves. The light turned to shadow the deeper in the tree line you went, so Samantha decided to stay in the open. The wind picked up some of the fallen leaves and moved them around like Mother Nature was redecorating the lawn. The grass was still very green, since it was early autumn, but there were splotches of yellow and brown here and there. She laughed to herself as she imagined Deacon pushing a lawnmower, wearing a sun hat.

She skirted around the cabin and was about to turn the corner that would bring her back to the front of the building, when she heard a chair leg scrape against the porch floor as if someone had moved it. The sound stopped her dead in her tracks. Deacon couldn't be back yet, and she would have heard Sebastion's car pull up the bumpy driveway.

"You don't have to be shy," a deep voice said from the porch.

She crept around the front of the house. The gravelly voice belonged to a man she didn't recognize. She jumped slightly in her skin as she debated about running back to the forest edge and trying to lose him in the shadows, but she knew she was in no condition to outrun anyone. The muscles in her legs fought against her decision to face the intruder.

He was sitting in one of the porch chairs as if he owned the place. He had one heavy boot resting on his knee as he reclined with his elbows propped on the wooden armrests. He was tall, and his muscles showed through the maroon T-shirt and flannel button-down he was wearing over tattered jeans. His sleeves were tucked and rolled up to just below his elbows, revealing crisscrossing tribal tattoos that disappeared under his shirt and reappeared from under his collar. His long brown hair stopped just below his shoulders. A touch of gray in his hair matched his sharp goatee.

"Don't worry." He smiled at her. "I don't bite. Often."

There was cruelty behind his false smile, and it scared her. His eyes glowed faintly as he continued to stare. The man took a cigar from his pocket and lit it with a match. The tip of the cigar glowed a bright red as he inhaled the smoke deep into his lungs and released it before he continued to speak. The wind blew the pungent odor toward her. It burned her eyes and turned her stomach.

"Of all places, I didn't think you'd end up here." His eyes moved along the forest's edge. He returned his gaze to her and smiled again. His sharp teeth were noticeable even from where she stood. She slid a hand over her throat as she imagined how they would feel puncturing her skin if he decided to attack.

"You seem to know me"—Samantha's stomach knotted as she spoke— "but I don't know you," she finished as she moved closer to the front of the porch. She kept her eyes trained on him and tried to sound brave.

"I'm crushed." He pouted. "I thought for sure Deacon would have mentioned me." He put his boot back down on the floorboards of the porch and leaned forward in his seat. His muscled arms were resting on his knees. Thick veins popped out on his neck as he rolled his head from side to side. He arched his brow as if he was sizing her up. Her heart lurched into her throat.

When Samantha didn't answer, he continued.

"Hmm…" He looked beyond Samantha, toward the road. "I guess not, then."

Her fight-or-flight response fought for control. She didn't know how far she would get, but it would be better than doing nothing. Running wasn't an option. She squared her shoulders and set her feet. She got the feeling he wasn't human. *Fight it is.*

"Please. Have a seat." He gestured for her to take the empty chair next to him.

"I think I'll stay right here if it's all the same to you." There was no way she was moving even an inch closer. If she didn't control her breathing, he would hear the terror in her racing heart. It didn't matter how brave she was on the outside.

He smirked as he took another long draw from the cigar and let the smoke drift slowly in the breeze. He shrugged his wide shoulders and put out the cigar on the surface of the little table next to him. "Have it your way," he said with a sigh.

Before she realized what happened, he was off the porch and was standing directly in front of her. He gave a mischievous grin. She jumped from his sudden appearance. He was a handsome man, but his features were dark. Evil emanated from him as he stood inches from her.

"Mmm…" He purred at her like someone would at seeing their favorite meal. "I can see why Deacon likes you so much." He ran the back of a large, clawed hand down the side of her face, causing her to step back from him, only to have him move quickly behind her. She bumped against his solid frame.

"What do you want?" The whole charade angered her.

"Oh, I want a lot of things," he whispered into her ear as he smelled her hair. His breath blew on the back of her neck. The sensation made her skin crawl as tiny hairs stood up all over her body.

"How did you know we were here?" Samantha asked. She had to keep him talking. All she needed was enough time for Deacon and Sebastion to return. Her heart lurched at the thought of them fighting against this monster.

His laugh vibrated through her. "I didn't expect to find *you* here. That was a bonus. Let's just say a little birdie whispered to me. I have eyes and ears everywhere."

"What do you want with Deacon?" Samantha tightened her hands into fists at her sides.

"I need to have a talk with him that's way overdue." He played with a strand of her hair, letting it slip between his fingers. "He was a helpful part of my pack once, and I guess you could say we had a falling out. He thought he could leave, and all would be forgotten, but I have an incredibly good memory." He grabbed a handful of her hair and pulled her toward him. "Maybe you could give him a message for me?"

"He'll be here any minute." Samantha steadied her breathing and forced as much bravado into her voice as she could. "Why don't you tell him yourself?" she sneered through clenched teeth.

He pulled tighter on her hair and laughed. "You are a wild one. Deacon and I have the same taste." His voice lowered. "I have other matters to tend to right now, so I need you to tell him, Kiren says hello and I'll be seeing him soon. We have unfinished business."

He stepped around to face her again while he held on to her hair. He pulled her head back to peer into her eyes. "You look so much like your mother. Has anyone ever told you that?" She narrowed her eyes. "No. I guess not."

"How do you know my mother?" She scowled.

"I can't say that I knew her well, but she looked a lot like you do now. It was a shame how she died." He frowned.

Samantha glared at him with disgust.

He continued to speak as he ran a clawed finger down the side of her face. His touch was gentle, but the sharp tip drew a small crimson line on her cheek. "She was brave too, like you, but bravery can get you killed under the wrong circumstances."

"Shut up!" she hissed at him as tears filled her eyes. She willed herself not to cry.

"Oh, come now." He pulled Samantha's face closer to his, causing her to grab his wrists. His skin was hot under her palms, and there was a deep scar running through his left eyebrow all the way down his cheek. "I thought we could be friends."

Samantha kept eye contact with him as he continued to speak.

"I wonder if Deacon would still love you if you were like us?" He tilted Samantha's head slightly to the left, exposing the smooth skin of her neck and shoulder. "There's a lot of perks to being a werewolf," he added as he let his teeth slide over her flesh.

"Go ahead," Samantha taunted. "You'll be the first

one I kill."

He laughed and pulled back from her neck to face her again. "You could be my queen." He smiled as he wiped the trail of blood away with his thumb. "I can only imagine the special abilities you would have then. If I changed you, you would beg to be with me. I can help you be free."

"What abilities?"

"I guess we'll have to wait and see." He smiled at her mischievously.

Like an answered prayer, a car moved down the bumpy dirt road, heading toward them. When Kiren released her, she turned toward the sound, leaving him standing behind her.

"Be careful who you trust, and remember to tell Deacon I stopped by. I will be seeing both of you very soon," he said to her back.

She turned to glare at him, but he was nowhere to be seen. She searched the area with her eyes, but he had vanished into thin air like a ghost. She bent at her waist and tried to stop the panic from taking over. Her head seemed to float separately from her shoulders as she straightened. Sebastion's car popped into view before she sat down in the dirt. She didn't know who Kiren was, but she knew he meant trouble, and she had no idea how they were going to get out of it.

Chapter 14

The hairs on Deacon's arms and the back of his neck stood on end as every nerve in his body fired, straightening his spine. If a werewolf ever followed an alpha, there was always a connection that continued to exist even if they broke from the pack. That presence grew the closer they got to his cabin.

"We have company." Deacon glared toward the unseen threat.

"What?" Sebastion eyed Deacon nervously. His eyes glowed as his hands shifted into claws. "Oh, that kind of company." He turned back to the road and tightened his grip on the steering wheel.

"Oh my God." Rhonda gasped from the backseat. "Sebastion, you can let me out here."

"I think you'd be safer inside the car," he said as he glanced at her shocked expression in his rearview mirror.

"Are you crazy?" she asked hysterically.

Sebastion slammed on the brakes as they pulled up on the cabin. Samantha was sitting in the dirt. Her pale face showed through the dust cloud as it settled. Deacon was out of the car and to her side in seconds. Before he was close enough to touch her, he instantly smelled his former alpha all over her. Adrenaline powered through him as he bared his teeth.

"Are you hurt?" he asked as he tried to control the violent beast within himself that was hungry for blood.

His claws dug into the flesh of his palms as he tightened his hands into fists.

"I'm okay." Samantha smoothed her hair with a swipe of her hand. Her eyes were wide and held a vacant stare.

Deacon opened his fists, allowing the punctured skin to heal. He helped her up and scanned the area with his sharp eyes.

"He's gone." She wrapped her arms around herself.

"Samantha!" Rhonda shouted as she got out of the car. She ran to her and pulled her into a tight hug. "I'm so happy you're okay! What's goin' on here?" She gestured toward Deacon.

Samantha hugged her back. Deacon ran around the cabin and into the tree line. "It's a long story."

"We should probably go inside," Sebastion suggested as he carried their bags from the car.

"Sebastion?" Samantha asked. "Who is Kiren?" His face fell at the mention of his name. Deacon jogged back to the cabin. They noticed his features had returned to normal, but his eyes were dark and brooding.

Sebastion gave Deacon a wary glance. An unspoken message passed between them.

"I know." Deacon scowled. "Let's move inside."

The warm cabin welcomed them. Rhonda joined Samantha on a small black leather love seat that sat opposite a matching sofa. The sound of the bags dropping on the floor made the girls jump. With an apologetic grimace, Sebastion dropped on the sofa and rubbed his hands over his head before Deacon broke the tension.

"What did he say to you?" Deacon asked as he kept his distance from them. He tensed as his fangs and claws pulsated. They craved flesh and blood as his anger grew. He could smell Kiren even with the distance he put between himself and Samantha. His nerves twitched in his muscles.

"He said to tell you that Kiren said hello, and he'd be seeing both of us very soon." He clenched his jaw and paced the floor as she continued. "He said that you both were overdue for a talk. What did he mean?"

"Did he say anything else?" Deacon asked. Samantha caught a glimpse of the blue glow in his eyes before he squeezed them tightly together.

"No," she lied. "That was all he said." Samantha was afraid to tell him the rest. She feared it would push him past his limit for tonight. Just being in the same area as Kiren's scent tortured him. With a nod of his head, Deacon left the cabin, slamming the door behind him.

"Would someone please tell me what's goin' on here before I lose my mind?" Rhonda asked the room.

Sebastion explained everything the best he could. Rhonda didn't believe him at first and accused all of them of being out of their minds, but after seeing Deacon's werewolf transformation and seeing the bruises on Samantha, she believed.

"And who is this Kiren?" Rhonda asked. "He sounds like a grade A asshole, if you ask me."

"He is," Sebastion said. "But he's so much worse than that."

"He said Deacon was in his pack once," Samantha pressed. "What happened?"

Sebastion didn't feel right telling them about Deacon's past, but they needed to know, and Deacon was in no way ready to talk about it with anyone.

"When Deacon was a teenager, he was persuaded to

join Kiren's pack. Kiren put it in his head that they would be able to protect people together, but he wanted Deacon because he was different from other werewolves. Kiren thought if he joined his pack, he could control him. He promised they would fight any hunters that threatened their kind, but what Deacon didn't know was that Kiren was a monster with a silver tongue." Sebastion paused as he recalled the story.

"So, that was the reason he left. I couldn't remember everything about that day." Samantha bit her lip as her eyes watered.

"Deacon found out the pack killed innocents, so he threatened to leave and return back to his family if they didn't stop." Sebastion took a long breath before he continued. "Kiren didn't like being challenged, so he took away anything Deacon had to go home to."

Tears streaked their cheeks as they listened to his story. "He killed his family?" Rhonda asked.

He nodded and swallowed the lump in his throat. "His parents fought back, so he killed them in front of him. That's where me and him met and my uncle Oscar. Deacon saved our lives that night." Sebastion's eyes were distant. "Deacon was stronger than Kiren realized. He was able to stand up and break his control over him. An alpha puts out this force over his betas so he can control them. It makes the pack work as one. I've never known a beta that can do that until that night. Deacon was born a werewolf. If Kiren had changed him himself, things might have ended differently."

"Did he kill my parents?" Samantha's voice cracked.

Rhonda placed a shaking hand over her mouth to stifle her sob.

"We don't know for sure. All we know is it was werewolves, but my uncle believes it was his pack."

"This is insane," Rhonda said. "Are you not freaked out by this?" she asked Samantha.

"I've remembered a lot from my past recently. I knew about werewolves and hunters before. My ancestors were hunters, but all this stuff about a prophecy…" She shook her head. "I won't let that happen. I won't become their weapon."

Samantha darted for the door. "I'll be back. I have to check on him."

Rhonda looked like she was about to protest but changed her mind.

The cool air washed over her as she stepped out onto the porch. She glanced at the chair Kiren had been sitting in, and a chill ran through her.

"He has that effect on people," she heard Deacon say. She found him lying back on the windshield of Sebastion's car.

Samantha took another deep breath and walked toward him. Clouds drifted across the darkening sky. The sun was already starting to set.

"Are you okay?" She was afraid to move any closer, but he seemed more in control. He wouldn't hurt her. That was something she was sure of.

His chest rose and fell with deep breaths. "His scent is all over you," Deacon said without facing her. He massaged the base of his skull as his body stiffened.

Samantha slid her hands over her neck as she remembered Kiren's touch against her. She stepped back a few feet and apologized.

"You have nothing to apologize for. I was trying not to get you involved. But I've failed."

"From what I've gathered over the past few days, it's more like I got you into this," Samantha corrected him.

Thousands of stars flickered to life as Deacon remained silent. The light of a tower blinked red in the distance.

"I'm sorry about your family." Samantha spoke softly.

"I'm sorry about yours." He blinked his eyes toward her.

She bowed her head and kicked at the gravel under her feet. She was still wearing his clothes. The collar of the shirt slipped off her shoulder as she shuffled her weight from foot to foot. His eyes roamed over her as she tugged the sleeve back into place.

With a deep breath, he unclenched his fists.

"I don't know how to feel about this. About my parents' death, I mean," she admitted. "I haven't remembered them yet. I'm not so sure I want to."

Deacon sat up on the hood of the car and let his legs hang over the curved fender. "We have to focus on the happy memories. If we dwell on the bad, it will only drive us further into the ground. You're on Kiren's radar now, but I will do everything in my power to keep you safe."

"I don't want you to get hurt because of me." Tears blurred her vision. She fought to keep her lips from trembling, but it was a losing battle.

He hopped off the car and pulled her to him. His strong arms wrapped around her. "Nothing's going to happen to me. It's you I'm worried about. I just found you again. If anything happens to you…"

She rested her head against his chest as her

shoulders shuddered. All the bravado she mustered earlier deflated as the tears fell. She let her mind empty as they swayed together in each other's arms. Crickets chirped in the background as an autumn breeze blew through the trees. This was where she was meant to be. For better or for worse.

Chapter 15

The next morning, everyone was adjusting as the shock of everything wore off. Samantha ran her fingers gently across the tender split in her lip. Rhonda returned to her spot on the love seat, a steaming cup of coffee sitting next to her on the coffee table as she scrolled through her phone. Sebastion flipped through a book in his lap as Deacon continued his watch by the window.

"I've got it!" Rhonda exclaimed as something on the small screen held her attention. "Michael McCray. He can help us."

Samantha's eyes widened. She couldn't believe she hadn't thought about Michael once since she last saw him at the hospital. Her cell phone was still in her employee locker. He would have the entire police force out searching for her.

"Michael McCray?" Sebastion closed his laptop and set it next to him. "I know I've heard that name before. Doesn't his family own half the town?"

"Yes!" Rhonda said. "He has people at the police station and all over. Samantha, what do you think? Would he help us if you explained things to him?"

All the eyes in the room were trained on her as they waited for an answer. The open space of the room slowly shrank in on her as her face heated. She flicked her eyes to Deacon, but her shame forced her to avert them. She remembered how badly Michael had reacted when she brought Deacon in to help save his life. She could only imagine how he was going to react to all this.

"He might find werewolves, hunters, and prophecies a little hard to digest," Sebastion stated. "What if reacts badly?"

"It'd be worth a try," Rhonda said. "How much worse could this get?" No one answered her, so she turned back to Samantha. "Have you talked to him since the other day?"

Samantha's chest tightened. Words scrambled in her mind, but her mouth wouldn't open.

"How do you know him?" Sebastion asked.

"We've been dating…for a little while," Samantha finally admitted. Deacon's eyes bore into her, but she couldn't bring herself to face him. Even with their history, she should have known better than to kiss him. It wasn't fair. Realization spread across Sebastion's face. He glanced at where Deacon was standing. His toned arms were crossed over his broad chest as he leaned against the far wall. His face showed nothing.

"I need to get my phone from the hospital and call Michael. I'll have to explain my absence somehow. It might as well be with the truth." Samantha stretched her legs and stood. "Sebastion, can you drive Rhonda and I to the hospital and then back home?"

Before Sebastion could answer, Deacon spoke up. "I can take you," he suggested. "If Sebastion doesn't care to take Rhonda home?" He met her eyes and didn't turn away.

"Uhm, yea. Sure." Sebastion pulled his keys from his pocket and fumbled them. He managed to catch them before they hit the ground. "I don't mind. If that's okay with you?" He gestured toward the front door.

"Fine by me," Rhonda replied. Relief washed over her face. One car ride with Deacon must have done her in. She eyed Samantha, giving her an unsure expression.

"I'll wait outside." Deacon spoke flatly as he walked out the door.

"So, Michael's your boyfriend," Sebastion said it as more of a statement than a question.

"Yes," Samantha said without meeting his eyes.

He gathered his things in silence, stuffing them into his messenger bag before following Deacon outside.

"What'd I miss?" Rhonda whispered to Samantha as the door closed behind him.

"We sort of had a moment." Samantha groaned. "Me and Deacon." She furiously rubbed her hands over her face and ran them down her hair with a sigh.

"Sort of?" Rhonda asked.

"More than sort of," Samantha said.

Rhonda's eyes grew wide as she gaped at her.

"We didn't do that!" Samantha exclaimed. She could practically read Rhonda's mind.

"Oooh," she said. "I didn't know. I just thought of Michael because I saw the reminder for his family's banquet tonight pop up on my phone. Are we still going to it?"

Samantha groaned and stared up at the ceiling. "I forgot about that. I'll call him and check in first, and then we can discuss everything at the banquet."

"You should have Deacon and Sebastion come too. Michael's going to have to meet him anyway, and it'd be helpful for Deacon if he had Sebastion there. Someone else he knows, ya know?"

"Are you sure that's a good idea?" Samantha asked.

"It'd be perfect." Rhonda clapped her hands

together. "There will be a bunch of people there, so Michael shouldn't freak out too bad. He'll have to stay calm."

"That doesn't make me feel very confident," she admitted.

"It'll work out." Rhonda grabbed her large purse from the floor. "Let's try to stay positive."

"Since when are you a positive Polly? You usually jump straight to the negative side of things."

"Since I found out werewolves exist, and there are people trying to turn my best friend into a weapon." Rhonda held open the front door. "I don't know how else to manage that."

She grabbed her backpack and met Rhonda at the door. Before she pulled it closed behind them, she cast a final glance at the cabin. She committed every detail to memory. Somehow, she knew this would be the last time she would see it.

Deacon was on his motorcycle as she stepped off the porch. Sebastion and Rhonda were loaded up in his car and heading back to town. Her heart raced as she stepped slowly to his side. He was wearing sunglasses and was leaning forward on the handlebars of his bike. Her reflection stared back at herself in his lenses.

"I should have said something before," Samantha confessed.

He leaned back and lifted a black helmet off the seat. "You don't have to explain anything to me," Deacon said gently before reaching the helmet to her. "You had to build a new life for yourself. I understand."

She swallowed the hard lump that formed in her throat. The cool outer shell was smooth in her hands. She picked at its fabric lining as she licked her dry lips.

"Hop on," he said as he scooted forward on his seat. He faced the cabin as the bike's engine roared to life.

Samantha swung her leg over the seat until she was straddling the cushion. She leaned forward to wrap her arms around his waist but hesitated.

"Hold on to me." His blue eyes were momentarily visible under the shade of the dark lenses as he cast a glance in her direction.

In order to wrap her arms around his waist, she had to scoot closer. His body was so warm and so right against hers. Her heart ached at the thought of never feeling that again. She thought she was happy being with Michael. He had always been so good to her, but being with Deacon was different. She wondered if the reason she hadn't thought about Michael since she was gone was because she didn't love him. She pushed the thought from her mind and focused on the road ahead. If the prophecy brought them back together, they should put as much space as possible between them even if it hurt to do so.

Once they reached the hospital, Deacon parked and offered to walk her inside, but she declined. She would be out soon. Hopefully, Bonnie, her supervisor, would be back and would see her injured face and believe the story she was about to tell her. If not, then she would be fired. Either way, this had to be done. She would have to call the bakery and tell Jake the same story. She couldn't believe how messed up her life had gotten in just under one week.

She ambled through the hallways until she arrived at the employee lounge that doubled as a locker room. Her clammy hand twisted the combination dial until the lock clicked open. She pulled her purse out and shut the door, not bothering to lock it back. Her cell phone was lost under all of the unnecessary items she'd piled in the mesh bag. The phone screen was full of missed calls from Rhonda, Michael, the hospital, and the bakery. She was about to call Michael, when the lounge door swung open, and Bonnie walked in.

She was her height and a bit heavier than her, but she carried herself well. She was wearing a white nursing jacket over pale orange scrubs that contrasted against her dark skin. Her brown hair was twisted in a bun at the nape of her neck. She pinned her with a fiery stare.

"Samantha! Where have you been?" she asked with a stern voice.

She turned, giving her a clear view of her face. The fire in her eyes cooled at the sight of her injuries. "What happened to you?" Bonnie moved closer and examined her bruises.

The details of the lie she had formed on the drive over here spilled from her lips. She hoped her appearance would be all the proof she needed.

"I went out of town for the evening the other day and ended up having another passing out episode, only this time, I fell down some stairs. I woke up at Saint Frances Hospital." Saint Frances was in the next town over. She hoped Bonnie wouldn't need them to corroborate her story. "If you could spare me for a few days more, I planned to follow up with my doctor and see if we can figure out what's going on. Dr. Franzin already took one scan after my last episode. I know it's late notice, and I hate to put you in a bind…"

Bonnie was still examining her face as she spoke. She let go of her and stepped back, putting her hands on her hips. "Yes. I spoke to Dr. Franzin. It would be a good idea for you to see someone. A specialist, maybe?" Her chest filled with air before she slowly released it. "That's fine. You've been here for years, and I don't think you've ever taken a vacation. You've been spreading yourself too thin." Her expression grew serious. "Is everything okay? Has Michael been treating you right?"

"Yea," Samantha answered. "He's been great."

She eyed her suspiciously but nodded. "Samantha, take care of yourself. You're one of the best nurses I've got. You work hard and are always helpful to all of us. Don't let anyone control you. Understand?"

"Yes. Thank you, Bonnie." Samantha assured her. "I'll take care of everything and will be back in no time."

"Let me know if you need anything. Keep us in the loop." She offered a small smile before she turned and left the lounge.

Samantha let out the breath she'd been holding in and followed her through the door. She managed to get back outside without running into anyone else. She called Jake as she went. He expressed concern but accepted her excuses. Lying didn't sit well with her as his words mimicked Bonnie's. She found Deacon pacing near his bike. His worried expression shifted to a blank one when he spotted her.

"How'd it go?"

"Well, I'm not fired. I'm on vacation or medical leave, I guess. Take your pick." She ran her hand through her hair, catching some of the wind-snarled knots on her fingers.

"A vacation sounds nice."

"I wouldn't call our situation a vacation."

"We could pick a different path. Point in any direction, and that's where we'll go." His eyes searched hers. She kept her emotions from showing on her face despite how badly she loved the idea. "Or not. Back to your place, then?" he asked as she climbed back on his motorcycle. The hope she noticed slowly dying in his eyes.

****

Deacon eased the bike into a parking space. They arrived at her apartment in no time. Samantha pulled the helmet off and shook out her hair. Chill bumps covered her arms from the cool wind as she rubbed her palms over them for warmth. "Thank you…for the ride."

"It was the least I could do." He shut off the engine and dropped the kickstand. The wind shifted direction, slamming her scent into him, turning the steel walls he had been trying to build around his heart to mush.

"You don't have to escort me." She held her hand up to his chest. Her cool touch and the firm set of her mouth shook him from his trance. "I can manage."

"I'd feel better if you let me walk you." She dropped her hand from his chest. He kept his face neutral. Samantha turned on her heel as a breeze tousled her hair. His keys dug into his palm as he tightened his fist around them. If he held them any tighter, they would've been crushed. He lifted his face to the sky as if he'd find the solutions to their problems there.

The pair ascended quietly as his thoughts raced. The familiar rosemary and mint fragrance of her apartment pulled them inside once she unlocked the door. The small space held dark shadows big enough for a grown man to hide in. Deacon searched the apartment and assured her there were no hunters skulking in closets or murderous alphas hiding under her bed. He met her by the door, but neither of them would meet each other's eyes.

"So, there's going to be a banquet tomorrow night. I would like you and Sebastion to come with us. It'd be good if you could meet Michael, and we could fix this. Together."

"Do you really think he can help us?" he asked. "This is a lot to take in for people who don't know things like me exist."

"Don't say it like that. You're not a *thing*. You're a good person. Just because you're a werewolf—" Samantha propped her hands on her hips.

"Ho won't understand." Deacon eyed the apartment, looking everywhere except for at her.

"He'll understand," Samantha assured him. "I'll make him understand. He really is a good guy. I think you'll like him. Will you come?"

The thought of having to play nice with this guy made Deacon cringe, but he would try to be on his best behavior. Her hazel eyes glistened with hope when their eyes met. He would do anything to make her happy. It wouldn't hurt to have someone like Michael on their side. "I'll go."

"Great!" Samantha said with a smile that stole his breath. It reached her eyes as they sparkled with excitement. "It's a black-tie event, I believe."

"I don't do suits," he said with an annoyed expression as he snapped out of her spell.

"It's a requirement. We could go together and pick something out for you if you want. It could be fun, and we all could use some fun, right?" she asked lightly as she shifted her weight on her feet.

He didn't think he knew how to have fun anymore. She chewed her lip and was holding her breath, waiting for him to answer.

"Okay. Sounds good."

Samantha stepped toward him as her hands twitched upward at her sides, but she stopped. "Rhonda and I could pick you up or meet you there? We'll be going to the mall."

"I'll meet you there. Just let me know the time." He needed to get out of her apartment before she smiled at him again. Another one of those and he would be fighting Michael for her hand rather than playing nice with him.

"Deacon, wait." She stopped him before he made it into the hall. She hugged him tightly. "Thank you for everything. You've brought back a part of my life that I never thought I'd see again."

He froze from the sudden impact. The wind from their bike ride had removed any trace of Kiren from her skin. He only scented her as he wrapped his arms around her protectively. Her sweet smell warmed him from within. He wished he could hold her forever.

"Stay alert and be safe," he whispered in her ear. "If you need anything, call me and I'll get here."

"I will." She pulled away from their hug. "The same goes for you. I'm here for you too."

He flashed a crooked smile as he peered into her eyes. He would always be there for her. He would come as soon as she called. It didn't matter what time or where he was, he'd find her, but that wasn't going to be enough.

"Good night." She held on to the door like an anchor.

"Good night." He left without another word.

He ignored the impulse that begged him to look at her once more. If he faced her again tonight, it would be his undoing. He took the stairs one at a time to let out some of the pent-up energy that had been building within him. A cool breeze washed over him after he pushed through the emergency exit door. His lips turned up into a smirk at the challenge that formed in his mind. May the best man win.

****

Samantha pressed her back against her door. She breathed in time with her ticking clock. Now that she had Deacon back, she didn't want to separate from him, even though her mind knew it was wrong. Her cell phone beeped in her pocket, reminding her the battery was about to die. She hooked her charger into the small device and sat on the edge of her bed, holding it in her hands. As she took a deep breath, she dialed Michael's number and put the phone to her ear.

It rang for a long time until Michael's voice came onto the line.

"Samantha!" His voice was frantic. "What's happened? Where have you been? I've been trying to reach you."

"I'm fine." Samantha explained what happened but left out all the supernatural details. She thought that was a conversation best left for in person.

His side of the call went quiet for a while. It was a lot to take in. She gave him time to digest everything. She tucked her legs underneath her as she waited. The mattress creaked from the movement.

"I'm coming over right now," he insisted.

"No, Michael, it's okay, really. It's late, and I'm exhausted. We'll see each other tomorrow, and we can talk then. I'm sorry I worried you."

"You're still coming to the banquet?" he asked.

"Yes." She twisted the charging cord around her

fingers. "I want you to meet Deacon. He's an old friend from before the accident. I invited him and another guy from work to come."

Michael blew air into the speaker.

She pictured him running his hand through his hair in frustration. "It'd mean a lot to me."

"That's fine," he said. "Try to get some rest. Tomorrow will be a big day for all of us."

"I will," she assured him.

"Good night." His smooth voice purred. "I love you."

Samantha paused at hearing those words but managed to reply. "Good night."

After they disconnected their call, she climbed under her blanket. She closed her eyes while her mind flashed between both of the men in her life. She needed to get a grip on herself if she was going to make it through tomorrow. She took a deep breath and released it as she tried to clear her mind. She didn't realize how tired she was until her head hit the pillow. Despite her thoughts running wild, she quickly drifted into a dreamless sleep.

The next day, Deacon met them at Glenwood's greatest attraction. The mall. It was smaller than the malls in bigger towns, but it had what they needed.

"I look like I'm about to make someone an offer they can't refuse," Deacon said more to himself as he modeled the suit Samantha had picked out for him to wear at the banquet. The small dressing room was like a coffin, and he was already wanting to change his mind about going. The pants fit good, but the shirt was constricting and not at all what he was used to wearing.

Deacon stepped out of the dressing room, and

Samantha's jaw hit the floor. The suit fit him perfectly. She chewed the end of the ink pen she'd been holding as she took in his appearance. Black was certainly his color. She admired how the charcoal-gray button-down shirt and black vest hugged his frame, showing off just how toned his body was.

He slid his hands down the smooth front of the jacket before removing it. He tossed it on a nearby chair and rolled the long shirtsleeves up to his elbows, showing perfectly toned forearms. The thought of his strong arms wrapped around her made her cheeks burn. He was always so warm, and he made her feel safe, but she had Michael now, and she needed to remember that.

She sighed and dropped her hands to her sides just as Rhonda strolled back to where they were standing.

"You better pick your jaw up off the floor too while you're at it." Rhonda chuckled as she plopped herself down on the opposite chair. She glanced over at Deacon, who was adjusting his sleeves, and shook her head. "Can't say that I blame you though."

Samantha jabbed Rhonda's arm with her elbow to get her to hush.

"I heard that," he said to them as he walked back into his dressing room. He flashed a crooked smile at Samantha's reflection in the long mirror he was using as he unbuttoned his shirt, elbowing his way past the privacy curtain. His icy blue eyes read her mind. The curtain closed swiftly behind him, leaving the two girls alone in the waiting area.

They faced each other in silence, already knowing what the other was thinking. "I know!" Samantha mouthed to her as she rolled her eyes.

"Uh, huh." Rhonda skimmed through an old

143

magazine she found by her chair.

Samantha was having doubts of her own about tonight. Maybe having him and Michael meet was a bad idea, but Deacon was the only one left from her past that she knew of, and until she could remember everything else, she desperately wanted him around. Michael would just have to understand that. If he truly loved her then he should see reason.

"Ready to go?" Deacon asked her as he appeared from the dressing room. He had changed back into his street clothes giving him a rugged look compared to the appearance the suit had given him. Her insides heated as her chest tightened.

"Ready as I'll ever be." She smiled nervously.

Chapter 16

Samantha spoke to Michael on the phone as they were leaving the mall. After some negotiating, he agreed to meet them at the banquet hall. He was silent for most of the conversation. She was going to ride with Rhonda to give herself time to think. Now that she was inside the large hotel, she wanted to run away. The room was filled with so many people she didn't know, and they were all dressed in their best dresses and suits.

"Calm down before you pass out," Rhonda whispered as she noticed Samantha nervously rubbing her hands together.

"I know." Samantha dropped her hands to her sides and breathed. "I'm trying."

"You can't pass out and leave me here with these people," she said as the crowd moved around speaking to one another. "That woman's outfit has to cost more than my car." Rhonda gestured to an aristocratic lady wearing a long, flowing black gown accented by white gloves and bright, shiny jewelry.

"After we talk to Michael, we can leave," Samantha assured her. "Have you seen Deacon and Sebastion yet?"

Rhonda stood up on her toes and searched the crowd. She pointed to the far side of the room. "There they are."

Samantha found them and was amazed at how much Deacon fit in here. The black suit was an excellent choice. He was smiling at the people that stopped to talk to him and Sebastion. As Samantha and Rhonda made their way over to them, Deacon met her eyes.

He did a double take when he caught sight of her. She walked gracefully toward him. She hated getting dressed up like this, but only did it for Deacon. The bright lights of the room added to the heat in her face. She was wearing a long, dark blue dress that had a slit running up one side. With each step, the dress revealed one of her smooth legs. The dress had long, sheer lace sleeves. The lace covered her chest just enough to remain modest, but low enough to make Deacon swallow hard.

Sebastion elbowed him slightly to get his attention back to the older lady that asked him how he knew the McCray family.

When Deacon returned to the lady, he coughed to clear his throat before he spoke. "We're old college buddies." The lady smiled and nodded her head to them as she made her way on to the next group of people. Deacon rolled his eyes at Sebastion. They needed to get out of there while they could. His suit jacket was smothering him, and everyone wanted to speak to him about things he had no idea about.

Sebastion was wearing a white dress shirt and a black tie with black slacks. His dress coat was slung over one shoulder. Sweat ran down his temple before he wiped it away with his sleeve.

"You're about to pass out too," Rhonda said as she stood next to him.

"What?" Sebastion asked as Rhonda broke through his thoughts. "Oh. Yea." He smiled at her as he tried to seem more at ease. His face turned a deeper shade of red. Rhonda's dress was orange with a black lacy trim around the bodice. It complemented the color of her skin perfectly. "You're beautiful."

"Thanks. It feels like something I wore to prom back in high school," she said with a laugh. "You're pretty handsome yourself."

Sebastion smiled and thanked her. "So, where are we going to do this thing?" he asked Samantha. "Have you talked to Michael yet?"

"I did." Samantha tried spotting Michael among the crowd. "I gave him the gist of what's happened, but figured we should tell him about the rest in person. I haven't seen him yet. I think that's him by the stage. I'll be right back." Samantha left her group and disappeared into the sea of bodies moving around the dance floor.

Deacon's face dropped once she was out of sight. His lips were parted as if he were about to say something but decided against it.

"It's going to be fine," Rhonda assured him.

Deacon gave a doubtful expression.

"See how well I'm taking all this." She raised her chin and grinned.

"Considering you already swung a bat at my head, threatened me with a butcher knife, and just about jumped out of a moving car to get away from me, that doesn't give me much confidence." Deacon pulled at the snug collar of his shirt.

"In my defense, I did the first two because I thought you were a burglar, not a werewolf." She nudged him playfully. "The jumping-out-of-the-car thing was understandable. Your little transformation took me by surprise. I'm cool now."

Deacon shook his head and smirked. "If you say so."

"I'm gonna hit up the drinks table." Rhonda squared

her shoulders. "Y'all want anything?"

"No but thank you." Deacon exhaled the breath he didn't realize he'd been holding.

Sebastion declined as well, so Rhonda moved into the crowd, leaving the two men to wait for their return.

"How do you think he's going to react?" Sebastion asked Deacon about Michael.

"Badly," Deacon answered. "There was a time when telling humans about werewolves was forbidden. I can't believe I'm about to do this. It's—"

Deacon froze and stopped speaking mid-sentence. Every muscle in his body contracted as the color drained from his face. He bent his head and turned it slightly as if he were trying to concentrate on something that caught his attention. He suddenly glared in the direction of the stage as his eyes glowed.

"What?" Sebastion asked him as worry laced his voice. "What is it?" He searched the room to try to find the source of Deacon's sudden alarm.

"One of the hunters from the warehouse. He's here." Deacon's gaze raked across the crowd.

"Are you sure?" Sebastion asked. "How do you know?"

"I caught his scent when they were chasing me. I've heard that voice before. We have to find the girls and get out of here."

Before they could move, Samantha reappeared from the crowd, holding hands with whom Deacon assumed was Michael. He was tall, and his dark hair was smoothed back from his forehead. As he and Samantha moved closer, Deacon realized the scent was coming from the man Samantha was pulling toward them.

"Deacon," Samantha said. "I'd like you and

Sebastion to meet Michael. Michael, this is Deacon and Sebastion. The guys I was telling you about."

Michael grinned at him. He stretched out his hand in greeting. "Nice to finally meet you face-to-face," he said without breaking eye contact with Deacon. "Hope you're both enjoying the party." His knowing eyes darkened.

Deacon hesitated before he took Michael's hand. His grip tightened as if it were a threat, before he slowly shook Sebastion's hand next. Sebastion flicked his eyes from Deacon's solemn expression to Michael's grin. They walked right into another unbelievably dire situation.

As Michael spoke, he knew he was the hunter that pulled the trigger on one of his own after he escaped the warehouse. Deacon met Samantha's eyes and wished she could read his mind, when Michael interrupted his thoughts.

"I guess I have you to thank for rescuing Samantha," he said, turning his mahogany-brown eyes back to Deacon. "I appreciate that." Michael grinned and pulled Samantha to him and kissed her gently below her ear before flashing a foxy grin.

It made his blood boil just watching Michael with Samantha. He held her like he owned her, and the sight made his claws and fangs pulse as he thought about ripping his throat out where he stood. There was nothing he could do in the crowded ballroom, so he tried to control himself. Their plan backfired. He needed to get the others out of here. If Michael's family were knitted all throughout the town, that meant there were hunters crawling around this whole place.

A man in a dark suit with a burr haircut walked up to Michael and spoke low in his ear, but Deacon heard everything. He coughed to get Samantha's attention. He edged closer to her and whispered, "We need to get out of here. Now. It's not safe."

Samantha pulled back from Deacon with confusion on her face. "What? Why?" She searched the room with a shudder. She held tightly to Michael's hand as anxiety showed on her face. She still believed Michael would be able to help them with their situation.

Michael nodded to the man that had approached them, before he turned back to the group. "I think the meeting room downstairs would be a better place to discuss this, don't you?" he asked Samantha as he kissed the back of her hand.

"You're probably right," she agreed.

"I think here would be okay too, though, right?" Sebastion interrupted, motioning toward a less crowded corner behind them near an emergency exit.

Michael faced Sebastion. "I really must insist," he said in a flat tone. Three men in black suits appeared behind them. Sebastion and Deacon exchanged worried glances. They were trapped. Trying to escape would draw too much unwanted attention.

"Do we really need all these bodyguards here?" Samantha asked Michael nervously.

"Just an extra precaution." He grinned. "I don't want to risk someone snatching you away from me."

Samantha nodded and searched Deacon's face. His eyes pleaded for her to know what he was thinking but couldn't say.

"Where's Rhonda?" Samantha asked them as she searched the crowd.

"We'll snatch her up later," Michael assured her as they left the ballroom.

Michael and Samantha led the way toward the elevators with Sebastion and Deacon behind them. The men who Deacon now realized were hunters were surrounding them. A bulge protruded from under the men's jackets that had to be a weapon. He planned to make his move as soon as they were out of the elevator. The ride to the floor below was slow as the tension built. Sebastion would be thinking of a way to get them out of this just like he was.

They heard the familiar ding as the elevator stopped and the doors opened. Michael stepped out with Samantha. He held her left hand in his left hand and had his right hand around her waist like they were about to dance, but as they cleared the threshold of the elevator, Michael tugged Samantha into his body and held tight to her hair.

Samantha screamed at the sudden shock of being pulled and having her hair twisted tightly around Michael's hand. "Michael!" she exclaimed. "Let go of me. That hurts."

"I didn't want you to miss the show." He smiled in her ear as he faced Deacon and Sebastion.

As Samantha met Deacon's eyes, the bodyguards shoved them out of the elevator. The three men closest to Deacon pulled out long cattle prods. The sticks came to life with electricity as they hit Deacon repeatedly. His muscles tensed as he fell to the ground by her feet. His face contorted in pain. His teeth and fists clenched as they continued to hit him with the electric prods until he stopped moving.

Sebastion hit the man nearest him with a sharp elbow to the face. Blood ran down the man's chin, but his attempt to help Deacon was stopped when Michael pulled a gun from underneath his jacket and pointed it to his head. Sebastion moved toward Deacon but stopped at the sound of the hammer cocking on the revolver. His face was red, and he was breathing heavily as he glared at him.

"Michael!" Samantha pleaded. "What are you doing?"

He slid his hand to the nape of her neck and turned her until her eyes met his. He lowered the gun to his side with a sneer. One of the other men put away his prod and moved behind Sebastion to zip-tie his hands behind his back. He flinched as they tightened the bindings.

"What I'm doing is my job." Micheal growled.

Realization spread across her face as she put everything together. Her stomach churned, and her heart dropped.

"You're one of those hunters?" Tears formed in her eyes. "You sent those men after me?" She couldn't believe she had been so naïve.

"Surprise!" he said to her with a cocky grin. "Thank you for bringing me these two. It saved me a lot of work." Michael noticed Deacon as he tried to rise up. He pushed Samantha toward one of his men and bent down next to him. "Especially this one." He pulled a small purple capsule from one of his pockets, and as Deacon lifted his head, Michael popped it open and released a fine purple powder. Deacon breathed it in and groaned with pain. His muscles tensed as he turned onto his back. He gasped for air as red spread from his neck up into his face.

His eyes glowed slightly before returning to their natural color. Dark veins streaked his pale skin. "What are you doing to him?" Samantha screamed. "Please!

Stop." Tears fell from her eyes as he passed out.

Michael's grin turned to a snarl as Samantha pleaded with him. He stood up from his crouched position. "He'll be fine, for now." He shrugged his shoulder as if this was an everyday thing for him. "This will make it easier for my men to move him."

"What should we do with this one?" The man behind Sebastion asked Michael as he held tight to his bound wrists.

Sebastion raised his chin as his nostrils flared. The closer Michael got, the more he could feel the hatred that flowed from him. "Bring him to my car." He glared into Sebastion's eyes, relishing the sight of his face turning red. "We'll take him and Samantha to the warehouse." He inched closer with a dark grin. "He can watch all of his father's research come to fruition."

Sebastion lunged at Michael but was caught short. Michael punched him hard in the stomach. He bent at the waist and coughed as he tried to catch his breath.

"Let's go," Michael ordered the men. Deacon lay motionless on the ground.

"No!" Samantha yelled as she kicked and struggled with the man that held her. "Let me go!" She bent at the waist and brought her head up quickly as it connected with his face. He let go of her long enough for her to run back to Deacon. He was barely breathing, and his eyes were closed. "Deacon!" she cried. "Please wake up!" But he didn't move. The other two men grabbed her then and zip-tied her hands behind her back. Their grip on her arms was hard enough to bruise as they pulled her away from him and down the hall. *This can't be happening!* She lost sight of Deacon around a corner. The smirk on Michael's face turned her blood cold.

Chapter 17

Rhonda spotted Michael and Samantha along with the rest of her group as they left the banquet room. She sat her drink down on a nearby table and followed them out of the room. It took longer for her to move through the crowd, and by the time she was in the hallway, they were leaving in the elevator. Deacon and Sebastion shared a worried glance, and she didn't like the fear she saw in their eyes as the elevator doors closed on them.

She waited to see what floor the elevator stopped at and decided to take the stairs down to see what was going on. She removed her high-heeled shoes so she could quietly run down the stairs without falling. Once she got to the door that led out into the hall, she slowly opened it. Samantha's scream froze her in her tracks. The sound of electricity crackled in the distance. She quickly closed the door and breathed heavily as a nervous sweat broke out over her skin.

"What the hell?" she said to herself. She took a few deep breaths. Her blood pounded in her ears. She couldn't stay in the stairwell, but her feet wouldn't move. Michael's voice echoed through the hallway, and she heard Sebastion groan. Footsteps grew closer to where she was. She ducked and hoped she wouldn't be seen through the small window in the door.

"What about the other one?" a man's voice spoke. She didn't recognize him.

"Rhonda?" Michael asked. "Send someone back down to deal with her, and be discreet. We don't want to interrupt the party."

She jumped from the crackle of a walkie-talkie as the man connected with someone else. She couldn't believe what she was hearing. Once the footsteps moved past her door, she slowly stood back up to peek through the window. Michael held Samantha's arm in a tight fist. Both she and Sebastion were tied at the wrists, but she didn't see Deacon.

"Please don't be dead," she whispered to herself.

Once she got her breathing under control, she snuck out of her hiding spot behind the door. The bright lights stung her eyes until they adjusted to them. She kept her back pressed against the wall as she tiptoed into the direction Michael came from. Her heart was beating so loud she was afraid they would hear it, but she pushed on toward the elevators.

She spotted a sign that pointed to her right with an arrow showing the elevators were right around the corner. Two men were speaking.

"Tie his hands," she heard one man say. "Let's get him up before someone comes down here."

Slowly, she peeked around the corner as she tried to keep herself hidden behind the wall. The men pulled Deacon up from the floor. His eyes were closed, but as they got him to his feet, he opened them just in time to see her. His eyes were unfocused, and he was struggling to stand.

At that moment, she lost her grip on the tiny straps of her shoes, and they clanged on the tiled floor. She pulled back from the corner and pressed herself against the wall with a curse.

"What was that?" she heard one of them say. "Go check it out."

The steady footsteps of one of the men approached her. Panic tightened her muscles, and the nerves in her fingers stung, but she forced it away. She was not about to get caught because she couldn't keep it together. She searched the hallway for anything she could use to defend herself. About fifteen feet from her, she noticed two crowd-control stanchions connected by a retractable red belt.

She ran as fast and as quietly as she could. She unhooked the red belt from one of the stanchions, but it slipped from her shaking hand and slid back into the other stanchion, causing a loud noise. She grabbed the stanchion before it could topple over onto the floor. As she hid in the shadows of the darkened room behind her, she waited for him to move past her. His stocky frame came into view, and she swung the heavy stanchion with all her strength. It connected with his face in a sickening crunch.

He fell onto his back, and his gun slid across the smooth surface of the floor. She hit him a second time to be sure it would be a while before he got back up. She picked up the dropped gun. The weight of the smooth metal in her hand was familiar. She used to practice shooting with her older brothers. Growing up in the South, a girl learned a thing or two, and right now, she was very thankful for that.

"Edwards?" the other man called out to his fallen comrade. With another deep breath, Rhonda hustled back to the corner that turned toward the elevators. She hoped she could take the other man out the same way she did with Edwards, but she was starting to lose her nerve.

She wasn't Jason Bourne after all. As the other man started to round the corner, she swung the stanchion with everything in her, but she misjudged where his head should've been. He caught the stanchion as it hit his chest and ripped it from her grip.

Deacon stumbled backward when the man released him. He fell against the opposite wall as his chest shuddered. He dropped to his hands and knees and shook his head.

"You must be Rhonda," the man sneered at her as he stepped closer, but he stopped as she pulled the gun on him. He was a foot taller and bigger than the other man and a lot scarier.

"Don't take one more step, or I'll unload this clip into you." She positioned her feet so she was ready for the kickback. Shooting at cans and deer were hugely different from shooting another human being, but if it meant protecting herself, she would not hesitate.

"Let me have that gun before you hurt yourself." The man smirked as he reached his open hand out to take the gun.

Her hand shook, and she backed up from him. "Not a chance." She squeezed the trigger, but her pause cost her. The man was fast and very well trained. He grabbed her wrist in his rough hand and pushed the gun toward the ceiling as it fired. Dust and plaster rained down on them. He disarmed her and had his hand around her throat, pushing her against the wall before she could fire a second round.

"I guess I'll be the one to dispose of you, then." His eyes were empty as he smiled down at her. "Let's have some fun first. What do you say?" He licked his lips as she struggled to free herself from his grip. Her eyes flicked to Deacon as he stood up behind him.

"I don't think so," she said through her gasps for air.

Deacon freed his wrists with a deep growl and hurled the man's body to the ground. Rhonda stumbled and fell to one knee before she caught herself. There was a faint rip at her side as the cool conditioned air touched her exposed skin.

The man tried to pull out his cattle prod to hit Deacon, but he was on him again in the blink of an eye. Deacon lifted the man from the ground and slammed him into the wall. His head bounced before he hit the ground in a loud crash. He was still breathing, but it'd be a while before he got back up.

More out of anger than anything else, Rhonda kicked the man as hard as she could. "That's for tearing my dress." She spat at his unconscious body. She hugged Deacon tightly. "Thank you!" Her lungs were burning, and her throat was aching.

He nodded and licked his lip, but before he could say anything, he collapsed. She moved in time to catch him as he went down to one knee. "You're not doing so good." His face was pale, and his neck was splotched with red. His eyelids drooped, and his chest shuddered against her with every ragged breath he took.

"Wolfsbane." He shook his head to clear his vision. "I'm…it'll wear off." He tried to stand back up, but he slipped. His voice grew hoarse from coughing. "We have to get out of here."

All his weight pressed on her shoulder. "I can't lift you. You have to help me. We'll do it together. Okay?" Deacon furrowed his brow in concentration as he agreed. "Okay, on three. One, two, three!" She grunted as they both got to their feet. "See." Her legs shook under the weight, and she could barely get the words out. "We've got this."

He laughed a little before the hearty sound was interrupted by his cough. He rubbed at his eyes and nose weakly.

"Think you can walk?" she asked.

"Yes." He stood more on his own two feet and wasn't leaning his weight on her as much. "Let's go."

They met a couple of older guests as they left the building. Rhonda assumed by their facial expressions they thought Deacon must be drunk. They exchanged smug glances before walking away. She found her car in the parking lot, and after unlocking the doors, she helped Deacon into the car.

She started the ignition before she had closed the door, and slammed her bare foot against the accelerator. The tires squealed against the pavement as three men ran out of the building after them. She caught a glimpse of one man talking into his radio before she slammed the gear shift into drive. She sped out of the parking lot and merged into the evening traffic. She put as much distance as possible between them.

"Rhonda," Deacon rasped. "You have to slow down."

She glanced at the speedometer and realized she was going way over the speed limit. Her panic held her foot in place. Both she and Deacon were breathing heavily as she chanced a glance at him in the passenger seat. With a deep breath, she slowed the car so they wouldn't risk being pulled over. He was resting his head back on the headrest with his eyes closed. "What's going on?" she asked him. "Who were those men?"

"They're hunters." Deacon wheezed. His face was

gray, and his hair was damp with sweat.

Rhonda divided her concentration between the road in front of her and Deacon. "Michael's one of them too?"

He shook his head. "He took Sebastion and Samantha."

"Took them where?" she asked. A car horn blared at her when she steered into their lane.

"I have an idea." He sat up straighter in his seat as he undid his tie and released the buttons on his collar. He fought with his jacket until he was free from it.

He shook his head and rubbed his hands over his face. She couldn't believe this was her reality. All she knew about werewolves was what she read about or watched in movies. "I keep thinking I'm going to wake up, and all of this would have been a bad dream. You're not supposed to be real."

"I wish it were just a dream. Everyone would be better off if I didn't exist." His eyes were facing forward as he watched the road. Deacon's lips parted slightly as sadness filled his eyes.

"I'm sorry. I didn't mean that. This has been a lot to take in." Rhonda pinched the bridge of her nose.

"And all this time I thought you were managing it pretty well." He repeated her words from earlier.

Rhonda let out a laugh that was both hysterical and relieved. "Right. I'm cool as a cucumber about all this." Tears lined her eyes. "This is all my fault."

Deacon's eyes landed on her hands. She was gripping the steering wheel so tightly that her knuckles were white. "This isn't your fault. You had no way of knowing Michael wasn't who he said he was."

"He better not hurt them," Rhonda said through a sob.

"He won't." Deacon cleared his throat. "Not yet. He can use Sebastion, and they need Samantha alive for the prophecy."

"This is so messed up." She wiped tears from her cheeks.

"We'll get them back," he said. "Both of them."

Rhonda peered into his blue eyes and nodded. She had no idea how they were going to do that, but she hoped they wouldn't be too late.

Chapter 18

From where Samantha sat in Michael's BMW, a large building appeared as the car drove over the next hill. She sat quietly next to Sebastion, leaving the town and their friends behind them. Michael leered at her through the rearview mirror. A smug grin stretched across his face.

"Don't beat yourself up." He turned his eyes to the road ahead. "We would've gotten him eventually."

The thought of Deacon hurt or worse made a lump form in her throat as tears stung her eyes. She led them into the murderous hands of their enemy.

She turned her eyes away from him and glared through the dark tint of her window. After they crossed the last hill, the road leveled out. The town's old school was just ahead. She knew where they were going. Michael's family owned a warehouse here that housed supplies to their businesses in town, but Samantha wondered what Michael really used it for. The building was once a factory but was no longer used as one.

The heavy metal doors loomed over the car as they rolled to a stop. The black SUV that escorted them parked, and more hunters stepped out onto the graveled path. She counted seven men, including Michael. They were pulled from the car and taken inside the tall building. The musty air filled her nose as the men hauled them inside. Large crates and other goods were scattered throughout the entryway. It was after they passed the last of the storage containers that she realized what this building was being used for.

Rooms were set up like gyms for training. There were rooms full of weapons, but the room they walked into next was different from all the others. It was a large empty space that might have once housed delivery trucks. Her heart threatened to leap from her chest, and her stomach dropped. An exam table was positioned in the center of the room next to equipment that reminded her of a mad scientist movie she previously watched with Rhonda. *Rhonda!* She said a prayer that she was safe as she met Sebastion's eye. Panic rose within her.

"It's going to be okay." Sebastion held her gaze.

"He's right." Michael walked ahead toward the table. "Once the procedure is over, you'll be stronger and more powerful. It will be a sight to see."

"I won't be a weapon for you to use to kill people," Samantha snapped.

"You won't have a choice." He closed in on her. "We'll be in control of who you kill, and as I'm sure you've figured out by now, Deacon gets the honor of being your first." He smiled down at her and moved her hair off her face. "Your first kill, anyway."

Samantha spat into Michael's arrogant face as her body pulsed with anger. Her blood boiled beneath her skin. "I would never kill him! No matter how much control you *think* you'll have over me."

Michael wiped her spit from his face with his sleeve before swinging his back hand hard at her face. The sound from the hit echoed through the room as she collapsed to the ground. The men gathered around them, taking in the scene. They laughed and murmured amongst themselves.

"Don't touch her!" Sebastion yelled at Michael as he tried to move toward him but was hit hard in the back of the head by one of the hunters' guns. He dropped to one knee as his warm blood ran down his neck. He blinked away the stars that floated in his eyes before glaring up at Michael. His face turned red while anger shook his body. "You won't get away with all you've done," he said through clenched teeth.

"Oh, but I have." Michael spoke as he rounded Sebastion. "I killed your parents." He kicked him hard in the face, knocking him to his side. "I found the chosen one." He continued as he repeatedly kicked Sebastion in the ribs. "And there's nothing you or anyone else can do about it."

Sebastion tried to block the blows to his core, but with his arms bound behind his back, he couldn't stop Michael from kicking him. He managed to roll over when Michael landed a final kick to his back. Sebastion fought to get air into his lungs. "And now." Michael ran a hand through his disheveled hair. "You get to watch me make my weapon." Sebastion coughed, and blood flew from his lips.

"Please, Michael!" Samantha cried. "No more. Please, stop this."

He stood above Samantha as she tried to stand. He gripped her arm with a tight grasp and ripped her from the floor. "This is going to happen with or without your cooperation." Michael spat into her face. Her busted lip ripped open after he hit her, letting blood run down her chin. Michael crushed his lips against hers. She struggled to pull away from him but couldn't budge. He stepped back and licked her blood from his lips.

"Get her ready," he shouted.

A man stepped forward and opened a door next to them. Supplies filled the deep closet from floor to ceiling. He removed a folded piece of fabric from one shelf. The man holding on to her pushed her forward, cutting the zip tie as they walked. She stumbled over her long dress from the force of his shove. She glared at both men as they tossed her the thin material.

"Change into this," the man by the closet grumbled.

"And if I refuse?" She glared at them.

One of the men standing by Sebastion cocked his gun and pointed it at his head.

"Any more questions?" he asked. There was no pity in his soulless eyes.

Samantha shook her head. Stomach acid churned and heated the back of her throat. With trembling fingers, she peeled off her dress and let the fabric drop to the dusty floor. She nervously tugged the hospital gown over her shoulders. It was close to see-through, and it was barely long enough to cover her. She was thankful that it at least tied on the sides. The gritty floor scratched and poked her bare feet.

"On the table," one of the men ordered.

"Samantha, don't," Sebastion pleaded. His face was red and coated with sweat as his chest heaved with fear and anger.

"I have to." She choked back tears. "They'll kill you."

"You know this is wrong!" he yelled at the men, hoping someone would stop this from happening. The man behind him holding the gun dug the barrel into his scalp. Sebastion blew out an angry breath as he forced his head to the floor.

Two men strapped Samantha to the table as the others moved the equipment closer to her. Vials of purple-and-blue liquid sat in a line next to a steaming vat of melted silver. Strange pipes and tubes connected it to syringes that glowed from the heat. Sebastion couldn't believe what he was seeing and worried how anyone could survive this torture.

Footsteps echoed behind him. He angled his head to see who was approaching. Michael returned with another man. He was short, balding, and wore thick glasses. His long white lab coat flowed behind him as they moved quickly toward Samantha.

"Good," Michael said to the room. "She's ready. Doctor?" He gestured to the man.

The doctor nodded and walked to her side. He examined every inch of her body, occasionally nodding and muttering things to himself. "She's perfect."

"Great," he said with a clap of his hands. "Shall we begin?"

"We shall. Are you ready, my dear?" he asked Samantha with a toothy smile. He didn't wait for her response.

The doctor pulled out sterile tubing and other medical equipment. Samantha's arms and legs trembled in her restraints as he neared her. She tried to move away from his touch but couldn't move far. She focused on the ceiling as the first needle pierced her arm. She bit her lip as tears ran down the sides of her face. Her lip bled into her mouth while the doctor continued his work. Once everything was secure, he faced the machine behind him.

"Let's begin," he said to the room as he flipped one of the switches and turned various dials and levers.

The machine buzzed, and terror gripped Sebastion

as scarlet liquid ran through the tubes. Samantha's blood filled a large, clear container and began to mix with the blue-and-purple liquid. He tore his eyes from the machine to Samantha. Her golden skin turned pale as too much blood left her body. Her chest rose slowly as he struggled to think of a way out of this. His pulse hammered in his ears.

Another piece of himself broke as he helplessly watched. He couldn't sit here and do nothing. They were running out of time. The container was almost full. The scarlet blood turned crimson and then darkened to black as the doctor operated various parts of the machine. He tried to stand, but the man behind him forced him back to his knees.

At first, Samantha lay motionless on the table as her enhanced blood began to pump into her body. A cold sensation hardened in Sebastion's stomach. She whimpered and tried to pull free from the table. The restraints held tight as she arched her back. The dark liquid coursed through her veins.

A force exploded from her body with a piercing scream, knocking everyone to the ground. All the lights flickered and went out, giving Sebastion the opportunity to break free of the ties on his wrists. He didn't waste a second as he moved toward the exam table. An explosion erupted somewhere in the warehouse just as his hands slid across the rails of the bed. The sound made his heart lurch into his throat.

"Get these lights back on!" Michael yelled in the darkness. "Check that out!" he ordered his men. "Are you able to proceed?" he asked the doctor.

"All we can do now is wait until the blood returns to her body before continuing the next step of the procedure." The doctor's words were dripping with nervous energy.

Sebastion was thankful the men were distracted, but he couldn't see anything in the dark room. The lights flickered as they tried to come back on. His ribs and back throbbed with every breath he took, but he tried to stay alert. The outline of Samantha's body on the table was dead still. At that moment, the lights flashed back on, and when Sebastion's eyes adjusted to the sudden brightness, he couldn't believe what he saw. Her eyes were glowing a shade of purple he recognized. The color reminded him of wolfsbane.

"She's magnificent!" the doctor said. "Are you ready to proceed?" he asked Samantha but didn't receive an answer. She was barely breathing as her eyes remained glazed. "Of course," he added, "this will hurt a bit." Before the doctor could turn back to the machine, Sebastion heard a monstrous growl that shook the molten silver and was followed by gunfire. He whipped his eyes toward the exit in time to see a man fly through the room. His body bounced once before skidding to a stop.

Deacon tore a pistol apart with his hands as he walked into the room. He was fully transformed and was heading toward them, when two hunters lunged at him. Without wasting another second, Sebastion jumped up and knocked out the doctor with one punch to his face, sending his glasses to the ground. Samantha's eyes were closed, and she wasn't breathing. The container that held her blood was empty.

He removed all the tubes from her body and quickly wrapped bandages around the injection sites. Blood smeared his hands as he worked. It wasn't the best bandaging he could do, but there was no time to make it perfect. More hunters were bound to barge in, and he and Deacon couldn't fight all of them. He released her from the restraints and tried to pick her up from the table, when a sharp pain shot through his ribs, knocking the air from his lungs. He winced and shook the dizziness from his head.

Deacon met his eyes as he struggled to move Samantha. The distraction gave one hunter the opportunity to slice a faint line across Deacon's abdomen with a blade. The man's eyes grew wide as his attack did nothing to halt Deacon. He landed a kick to his chest, sending him tumbling backward. He hustled to Sebastion's side.

"I can't lift her." He groaned. "My ribs." He coughed again and spit out more blood onto the floor.

Deacon ran his hand over the bandages on Samantha's arms and neck before facing the machine. He bared his teeth at the bubbling mixture of melted silver. His eyes glowed brightly as he pulled the machine over onto its side. Sparks flew from it, and the silver coated the floor. He turned back to Samantha and gently slid his arms under her back and legs. He held her tight against him.

"They didn't finish the procedure, but they came close. How do we get out of here?" Sebastion asked.

"This way," Deacon spoke as he led him out of the warehouse. "There's a hidden tunnel. I used it last time I was here."

Once they were far away from the building, Sebastion had to stop. His chest burned like fire, and his head began to swim. "I'm sorry," he said between ragged breaths. "I need a second."

"We don't have a second. Come on," Deacon urged

him. "We're almost to the car."

He nodded and tried to catch his breath. He followed Deacon until they spotted Rhonda's car. He opened the door to help him slide into the backseat with Samantha. Deacon held her in his lap as he handed Sebastion the keys. Sebastion jumped behind the wheel and turned over the ignition.

The car roared to life as Deacon was trying to wake up Samantha. "She's not breathing." His brows were knitted together as he held her lifeless body in his arms. He strained his hearing, but there was no heartbeat.

Sebastion floored the gas pedal, causing tires to spin gravel as he peeled out. The car slid from side to side, almost skidding into a ditch before he gained control over it. He heard her gasp as she took in a large breath of air.

"Is she awake?" He swerved the car back onto the road.

Her breathing leveled out. She was trying to open her eyes. "Deacon?" she asked in a hoarse voice.

"It's okay," he assured her as he held her close. "You're safe," he said to her as her head dropped to the side.

"Is she okay?" Sebastion's voice rose with panic.

"She's breathing, but she passed out." Deacon caressed her cheek. The tightness in his chest eased with every breath she took.

Sebastion sighed and took control of his driving. "How'd you get away?" Sebastion asked him. "And where's Rhonda? Did she make it out?"

"She's fine. She saved me." Deacon laughed. "I owe her."

"I'm going to marry that woman." Sebastion

cheered as relief filled him. They got away, and the hunters couldn't finish the prophecy. "Where to?"

"To Oscar's cabin," Deacon instructed him. "He's back in town, and he'll need to examine her."

Sebastion nodded his head and took the exit that led to the interstate. Oscar's cabin was in the city limits of Glenwood, but it was so off-the-grid it was difficult to find unless you knew where you were going. Sebastion relaxed in his seat as he drove through the darkness of night. He would take their small victory and leave the worrying for tomorrow. He stole a quick glance at Deacon in the rearview mirror. His face was serene, and his eyes were bright as he combed his fingers through Samantha's hair. He hoped she would be okay. If Samantha were to die, Deacon would die along with her.

Chapter 19

Thunder clapped, jolting Samantha awake. Panic rippled through her chest as she imagined the straps were still around her wrists, only to realize she wasn't bound. She searched the dim room and tried to focus. Her vision was blurry but was improving. She pressed her palms into her eye sockets and rubbed them until small burst of light appeared from the pressure. A cool hand touched her arm.

"Samantha." Rhonda's voice calmed her.

Her blurred image sharpened when she pulled her into a tight hug. "You're okay!" she exclaimed as her voice cracked. "It was Michael." She pulled back from their embrace. "He's a hunter. He's—"

"I know," Rhonda interrupted as tears welled in her eyes. "I followed them and found Deacon. We got out, and he brought us here."

A creaky floorboard caught Samantha's attention. Deacon was leaning against the doorjamb. "Where are we?" she asked, as she didn't recognize her surroundings.

"Sebastion's uncle's place." Rhonda squeezed her hand. "This is his cabin. His name is Oscar. You've been out of it for a while."

Her throat tightened, and her heart dropped into her gut. "Oh, no...Sebastion!" Tears dripped from eyes as she jumped up from the bed. "Where's Sebastion? Did he make it out? Oh…" She covered her mouth before a sob could escape.

"I'm here." She heard Sebastion's voice as he stepped slowly into the room.

Relief washed over her. He was bare from the waist up. His ribs were wrapped tightly with an elastic bandage. Purple and blue bruises were scattered across his light skin. His left eye was black and swollen, and he had a busted lip. Light bounced off a small cross necklace he wore around his neck. She closed the distance between them and hugged him gently. She tried avoiding the worst of his bruises. He winced but didn't pull away.

"I'm glad you're safe." Samantha cried into his shoulder. "All of you. I'm so sorry. This is all my fault. I should've known."

"This isn't your fault." Sebastion rubbed her back until Deacon stepped in.

"How are you feeling?" Deacon asked.

She wiped the tears from her face. She caught Sebastion's hand and gave it a little squeeze before he sat stiffly in a small chair near the door. She took inventory of her own body.

"I feel…great, actually." She gave a small laugh.

Deacon's eyes combed over her face in awe.

"What do you remember?" he asked cautiously.

Samantha concentrated on the floor as she filtered through her memories.

"I remember the banquet and being brought to the warehouse." She remembered the beating Michael gave Sebastion for defending her. It was something she would never forget.

"Anything else?" Deacon asked.

"They strapped me to an operating table. I remember starting to feel cold. I could barely stay awake and then…" She shuddered. "There was pain. I was on fire. Did they…" Her mouth grew dry as she searched for the words. "Finish it?"

"No." Deacon held her trembling hands in his. "They started it, but we got you out before they could."

She sighed with relief and sat back down on the bed. She cradled her head in her hands. In the distance, a door slammed closed as someone else entered the room.

"Ah. She's awake at last." A man she assumed was their host entered the room.

"This is my uncle, Oscar Walsh." Sebastion introduced the stranger. "He's a hunter."

Samantha's eyebrows rose at that as she eyed the stranger.

"He's one of the good guys." Deacon assured her with a smile.

Oscar was of medium height and build. His hair was cut short, and she noticed subtle grays running throughout his dark waves. His eyes were similar to Sebastion's. There was a strong resemblance between them. He dropped more pieces of wood next to the fireplace before dusting off his gloved hands and walking over to where they stood near the bed.

"Let's see how you're healing." He pulled off his gloves and knelt next to the bed. He examined her face and removed the remaining bandages. He smiled, but she caught a glimpse of concern in his dark rosewood eyes. "You're completely healed."

"How long have I been here?" Samantha asked as a feeling of déjà vu crept into her mind.

"A couple of days." Oscar folded the bandages and

tossed them aside. Her mouth turned downward, and her eyes stung as her anxiety grew. "Since they were able to start the procedure but not finish it, you may start to experience some…changes." His eyes flicked to Deacon's before returning to hers.

"Changes?" Samantha asked with wide eyes. "What kind of changes? I'm not going to grow a third arm, am I?"

Oscar laughed. It was a deep and warm sound that soothed her nerves. "No. Nothing like that." He stood up and moved to a nearby bookshelf that held rows of old books. The spines were worn from use. He removed a dark red book with gold trim from the top shelf and brought it to them. "There's a lot we don't know for sure, so we'll have to wait and see, I'm afraid. The last time anyone tried to pull off something like this, it was a thousand years ago, and they didn't get as far as Michael as far as we know."

"But I feel great." Samantha's brows bunched together as she glared at the book in his hands.

Oscar read to himself before meeting her eyes. "One thing is for sure. You can rapid heal."

Samantha laughed but noticed the seriousness on everyone's face and remained quiet. She licked her lips as she tucked her hair behind her ears. She shivered despite the warmth from the fireplace nearby. The hospital gown left her feeling exposed. As if he read her mind, Deacon wrapped her in a blanket. His warm hand moved down her back before he stepped away.

"You don't have a bruise or a scratch on you." Rhonda's eyes were wide as she spoke.

Samantha darted into the bathroom and examined herself in the mirror. The skin on her face was smooth and appeared normal in the bright lights. There were no bruises, and her lips were unchanged. She examined her arms, but there was nothing. Instead of resembling someone's punching bag, she looked completely ordinary.

Samantha turned off the light and walked back into the room to join the others. She pulled the blanket tight around her. "What else is going to happen to me?"

Deacon and Oscar shared a concerned glance.

"You may develop abilities." Oscar spoke carefully, but she could tell there was something he wasn't telling her. Dust floated from the book when he clapped it closed in his hand.

"Like what?" she asked.

"Telekinesis, for one." He returned the book to its place on the shelf. "To be honest, your powers could be limitless or might stop at being able to heal yourself. The fact is we don't know for sure, but—"

Deacon kept his eyes trained on the floor. His arms were crossed tightly over his chest as the muscles in his jaw ticked.

"What is it?" she asked them. "What aren't you telling me?"

Oscar scratched his groomed beard before meeting her eyes. "The prophecy states that if the procedure is started but not completed, then the host would die."

She couldn't believe what he was saying. "But I feel better than ever."

"Yes. You feel fine now." Oscar tried to explain. "You have until the end of this last blood moon, and if the procedure isn't completed, I'm afraid…"

"We've been researching alternatives." Rhonda scooted closer to her side.

"We're going to try everything we can." Oscar promised, but his eyes didn't show he believed it.

"We won't let you die," Sebastion promised. His face was set as his dark eyes turned glossy.

Samantha appreciated their optimism, but her gut twisted. There was nothing they could do but wait.

Chapter 20

The next morning brought them a warm and cloudless autumn day. The sunlight shone brightly through the open windows of Oscar's cabin as Samantha moved to the bathroom next to the guest room she was using. The cabin was quiet. She assumed everyone was outside enjoying the nice weather. A few days had passed since she woke up here, and she was excited to have a hot shower and the largest cup of coffee she could get her hands on. With a stretch and a yawn, she pushed open the bathroom door.

"Ah!" Samantha turned her eyes away from Deacon as soon as she spotted him standing in front of the vanity wearing only a towel. He removed his toothbrush from his mouth and swiped a spot of toothpaste from his lip with the back of his hand. "I'm sorry. I didn't think anyone was in here."

He laughed at her reaction as he rinsed his toothbrush under the faucet. She turned back to face him. She loved hearing him laugh more than anything, and now she couldn't help but admire his other great qualities. Beads of water rolled down his back from his wet hair and were absorbed by the plush, green towel that was wrapped low around his waist. She was tracing the lines of his muscles, when she noticed him watching her in the mirror, causing her face to warm.

"Well, if you're done in here, I'll hop on in the

shower." She crossed her arms in front of her as she waited for him to leave.

"Hop on in," he said with a sly grin. "I'm almost done."

He shook a small aluminum can and put a glob of the foamy, white shaving cream into his hand. She regarded his reflection with a raised eyebrow.

"I won't peek. I promise." His smile turned playful.

She shook her head and slid past him, careful not to brush against his body. She undressed quickly and hopped into the shower, closing the crystal door behind her. In her haste to start the shower, she turned the chilly water on by mistake. She jumped as the cold bit into her hot skin.

"Are you okay?" Deacon asked.

"I'm okay," Samantha said quickly as she fumbled for the hot water. "I didn't realize the showerhead would come on first." His outline was etched in the crystal door, and his restrained laughter echoed in the small area. "It could happen to anyone," she said in her defense.

"Oh yea. It can." Deacon tried to hold in another laugh.

She welcomed the hot water as it splashed her face and coursed down her body. She rubbed the water from her eyes, letting the force of the shower beat against her back. She decided the better choice would be to make it quick. She didn't want to risk anything else happening to embarrass herself in front of Deacon. She washed her hair and ran the conditioner through it, hoping that it would release the tangles. She mentally thanked whoever it was that put her toiletries in the shower for her.

Once she rinsed away all the soap and conditioner, she turned off the shower and squeezed as much water from her thick hair as she could, when she realized she forgot to grab a towel. She stood glaring at the high ceiling of the bathroom before facing Deacon's silhouette through the door.

"Deacon?" she asked with a sigh as she slid her foot through the water at her feet. "Is there an extra towel out there by chance?"

"Yea." His shadow moved slightly. "I've got one."

"Great!" Samantha smiled as she cracked the door to grab it. Deacon was holding a green towel in open arms, ready to wrap around her. She paused before stepping out of the shower toward him. He kept his eyes on hers as he wrapped the warm towel around her wet body, keeping his promise not to peek where he shouldn't. He leaned in close and breathed on her shoulder. The sensation made her skin chill, causing her breath to catch in her throat.

He pulled away and tucked the top corner tightly into the fold at her breast. He gently tucked a loose strand of hair behind her left ear. The touch of his fingers against her flesh sent fire shooting through her core. His scent mixed with the floral shampoo and body wash that swirled in the remaining steam from her shower. They held each other's gaze while the fog enveloped them.

"Thank you." She spoke in a faint voice. Being so close to him made her heart race.

"My pleasure." He gave her a crooked grin as his eyes darkened.

He ran his hands down each side of the plush towel, smoothing out its wrinkles. His warmth soaked through to her as she committed every detail of his smooth face to memory. He shifted his gaze from her lips to her eyes. She noticed the splinters of turquoise scattered throughout their usual clear blue. Samantha brought her hand slowly to the side of his face and traced the line of his jaw with her finger before flattening her palm on his toned chest, feeling his heartbeat underneath.

He held her hand in place and brought his free hand up to hold her cheek in his palm. She savored the feeling as she nuzzled her face into it. He closed the gap between them while her eyes were closed. As she opened them, his eyes dropped to her lips. His stare held a question as if he were asking for her permission.

She answered him by moving closer until their bodies were touching. He held her waist in his strong hands as he pressed his lips to hers. His kiss was gentle at first until her breath caught in her throat. She pulled him tightly against her. In two steps, he pressed her against the wall as their kiss deepened. When they pulled away from each other, his striking eyes glowed brightly in the natural light in the bathroom.

"Are you afraid?" Deacon peered through to her soul, searching for any sign that he should stop.

"No." Samantha ran her hands through his wet hair. "Should I be?" she asked him with a sensual smile.

Deacon returned it with one of his own that took her breath away, causing his eyes to glow brighter. Her heart raced as he kissed her shoulder and moved slowly up behind her ear. Heat shot through her belly with every contact of his lips until she heard the front door of the cabin open and slam shut.

"Hey, Deacon!" Sebastion shouted from the living room. "You almost done in there?"

Deacon pulled away from their kiss and glared at the ceiling. She watched him shake his head at the interruption. She couldn't help but smile and had to cover her mouth with her hands to keep from laughing.

"I think I'm going to kill him," Deacon whispered to Samantha as she tried to hold in another laugh.

"Have you seen Samantha?" Sebastion asked through the bathroom door. "Rhonda was needing her."

Deacon grinned as he traced the edge of her chin with his thumb. "Yea. I saw her."

"Well?" Sebastion asked as he waited for more information.

"I'll be right out." He rolled his eyes before kissing her on the forehead, giving her another breathtaking smile, before leaving the room.

"You take the longest showers," Samantha heard Sebastion tell him when he walked out of the bathroom.

Sebastion stepped into the room, carrying his toothbrush in one hand and had his towel draped over his shoulder. His expression changed to shock as he spotted her standing in only a towel. He gaped at Deacon as he disappeared into another room, before dropping his eyes to the floor.

She couldn't help herself. She busted out laughing at them.

"I am so sorry." Sebastion kept his eyes down. His cheeks turned pink.

"It's okay." She tried to control her laughter. "Deacon was shaving, and I just got out of the shower."

"You don't have to explain anything to me." He traded places with her so she could get to the door. "I need no details."

Samantha smiled at him as she closed the door behind her, separating them. He muttered something about the cabin being too small and something about having only one bathroom not working out. She couldn't help but laugh again, and with everything that was going on, she realized how nice it was to feel this way. She hoped there would be more days like this, and with a smile on her face, she went to her room to get dressed.

Chapter 21

When Samantha came out of the guest room, she followed her nose that led her straight to the coffeepot. It was sitting on the marble countertop in the small kitchen. She loved the smell of coffee brewing and couldn't wait to enjoy the hot beverage.

"Sorry if it's too strong." Oscar came into the kitchen with an empty mug. "I only know how to make it one way."

She smiled as she swallowed her first sip of the dark brew. It was stronger than she was used to, but she welcomed the warm sensation as it spread in her stomach. "It's perfect." She hoped her smile showed him how grateful she was for everything.

He nodded before lifting the decanter, refilling his *World's Greatest Uncle* mug.

"A gift from Sebastion?" Samantha pointed to the small cup in his hand.

Oscar read the writing on its smooth, white surface and smiled. "Yea." He laughed. "I have the shirt to match." Wonderment filled his eyes. "How are you feeling?"

"I feel great." She sipped her coffee as her mind pondered on Michael's betrayal. It was all she could think about since the incident.

"You couldn't have known about Michael." Oscar read her mind.

Samantha smiled nervously. "Am I that easy to read? I should've known something wasn't right. I trusted him."

"You can't beat yourself up." He leaned against the counter before taking a hearty sip of his coffee. "Men like Michael are good at deception. I'm sure he's tricked a lot of people. It is what it is. That's what Sebastion's mother used to always say." Pain flashed in his eyes for the loss of his brother and sister-in-law at the hands of Michael and his lot.

"I'm sorry." Samantha wiped a dark brown drip that was running down the side of her mug.

"It's okay." Oscar assured her with a smile. "Let's not dwell on the past. Come on outside." He gestured toward the front door. "I think Rhonda has the party all set up for us."

"Party?" Samantha followed him. "For what?"

"You'll see." Oscar smiled as he led her into the backyard.

Samantha followed him around the cabin until the smell of bacon frying reached her nose. She didn't realize how hungry she was. As she cut the corner that led to the small patio, she spotted balloons and a small HAPPY BIRTHDAY sign. The sun glinted off the metallic letters.

"Surprise!" Rhonda yelled as soon as she spotted them. "It's not much, but we did the best with what we had."

Her eyes widened as she covered her mouth. With everything that had been going on, she forgot her own birthday. Light filtered through the colorful balloons as the wind swayed them. "You didn't have to do this."

"I wasn't about to let your birthday go by without a

celebration." Rhonda hugged her tightly.

"Happy birthday!" Sebastion sang as he brought out a stack of pancakes with a candle on top. "We didn't have cake ingredients, but pancakes are a close second, right?" He sat the plate down on the picnic table in front of her and smiled. "Make a wish."

She committed each of their faces to memory. She was so moved at their acts of kindness that tears filled her eyes. She stopped when her eyes fell on Deacon. He was leaning against the cabin and was trying to hide a bashful smile. "You knew about this?"

"Sort of." He shrugged as a wide smile spread across his face, creating butterflies in her stomach.

"Don't let him lie to you." Rhonda moved a low-hanging streamer out of her face. "He hung all the decorations at six o'clock this morning and made the pancakes."

"You can cook?" Samantha eyed him suspiciously, but he only shrugged.

Everyone laughed as they gathered around the picnic table to watch Samantha blow out her candle. She knew what she would wish for. She took a deep breath and put all her hope into her wish before opening her eyes and blowing out the little flame. They clapped, cheered, and wished her happy birthday again before sitting down to dig into their breakfast.

The day seemed to fly by as they talked, shared funny stories, and joked with each other. As the sun dropped low in the sky, the patio lights clicked on around the small backyard. The sun disappeared behind the trees; she was happy to see that only stars remained in the now-dark sky. It was a relief not to see the moon, even though she had always loved basking in its bright glow. The moon no longer held the same feeling for her.

"You're not supposed to be sad at a birthday party," Deacon said as he brought her a thin jacket. He helped her slip her arms into the soft material. His fingers slid down her arms, causing her heart to skip a beat.

"Thank you. For all of this." Samantha admired the small lights that lined the patio. "It's perfect."

"I would do anything for you as long as I get to see your smile," Deacon admitted as he held on to the edges of her jacket.

"That's the best line you've got?" Sebastion carried a small karaoke machine and sat it down on the picnic table.

Deacon turned his eyes to the sky and sighed before giving Sebastion a death stare.

"Don't kill him." Samantha cupped his elbows in her palms.

"He's pushing his luck." Deacon shook his head before meeting her gaze.

"I can take him," Sebastion said over his shoulder as he hooked the small machine up to a bright orange extension cable.

"You can, can you?" Deacon swaggered toward him.

"Yea. At karaoke." Sebastion tossed him a small, black microphone.

"I don't sing." Deacon turned the device in his hands.

"What?" Sebastion grinned. "You scared?"

He rolled his eyes and turned to face Samantha who was doubled over laughing. "This is the only time." He pointed at Sebastion. Rhonda and Oscar moved in to watch their performance.

As Samantha got control over her laughter, she joined them. They had the best seats in the house as Deacon and Sebastion serenaded them with their best attempt at a Sonny and Cher song. By the end of the first chorus, Deacon gave up and turned the microphone over to Rhonda, who was happy to finish it. They sang two more together until they offered her the microphone.

"No way!" Samantha dried the tears of laughter from her cheeks. "I'm perfectly fine being the audience," she said as a slow song started to play from the speaker.

"I know this one." Oscar set down his drink and stood up. Rhonda handed the microphone to him, but he sat it down. "I'm not the singer of the family, but I have been known to cut a few rugs." He smiled as he held his hand out to Samantha. "Shall we?"

"I'd love to." Samantha smiled and took his hand. They stepped hand in hand to the center of the patio and swayed to the slow beat. He twirled her away from him and then pulled her back as he dipped her. She laughed as he continued to dance her around the yard. As the beat picked up, she noticed Sebastion and Rhonda had joined them. They moved to a beat of their own.

There was a short pause in the music until a slow rhythm drifted toward them. Samantha thought it was an Elvis song but wasn't sure. At that moment, there was a tap on her shoulder.

"May I cut in?" Deacon held his hand out to her.

"You may." Oscar kissed Samantha on the cheek and bowed out with a smile.

Her cheeks ached from smiling but welcomed it. Oscar took back his spot at the picnic table as Deacon pulled her toward him for their dance. He held her hand in his while his other hand rested on her hip. They swayed together as the song played in the quiet of night. "This has been the best birthday I've ever had."

"I'm glad." He pulled her close to him as she rested her head on his shoulder. His voice deepened as it vibrated through her. He sang softly into her hair along with the melody. She pulled back with surprise. "You can sing."

"Don't let Sebastion know." He grinned.

She shook her head and glanced over at Sebastion. He was holding Rhonda as they swayed back and forth to the sweet song. The sight of her best friend and her new friend together filled her with joy. She hoped after everything was over, they could be like this all the time. She was happier and more at ease in that moment than ever before. If she could make another wish, it would be to have more birthdays like this. Deacon wrapped his arms tightly around her and rested his chin on her head. She closed her eyes and listened as he sang softly in her ear.

Chapter 22

Samantha woke the next morning feeling full of life and energy. Getting older should give her anxiety about wrinkles, but she had the best birthday and wasn't about to let worry ruin her mood. She stretched her arms and legs as she surveyed the backyard. All the decorations had been removed, and everything was pushed aside to open the area for their first training session. Deacon stretched his shoulders and flexed the muscles in his arms.

"Your training should come back to you the more we practice," he assured her.

She took a deep breath and stepped into the yard feeling like she was trying out for a sports team. Rhonda and Sebastion joined her as Deacon and Oscar brought out the practice gear from the small shed that stood beside the cabin. Deacon wore a black T-shirt that hugged his torso in all the right places.

"Okay. Sebastion, you pair up with Deacon to show the girls what we'll be practicing today," Oscar instructed.

Deacon grinned at Sebastion. He'd take this chance to get back at him for all the times he'd interrupted their moments together. After glancing at Samantha, he laughed. It was a secret they held just between them. Sebastion raised an eyebrow at them, which only made them laugh harder.

"I'll go easy on him," Deacon promised.

"Don't feel like you have to hold your punches with me." Sebastion squared his feet to face him.

"Remember, this is just practice," Oscar warned. "We'll start with some hand-to-hand combat first." He took a seat at the picnic table that was pushed against the cabin so he could watch and help as needed. "Whenever you're ready."

The yard was quiet until Sebastion went in for the first attack. Deacon was quick to block his punch and managed to flip Sebastion over onto his back.

"Did you not hear him say *practice*?" Sebastion wheezed from the ground.

"Did *you* not say for *me* not to hold my punches?" Deacon countered with a grin as he walked around him.

Once Deacon was at his side with his back to him, Sebastion quickly swiped his leg across the grass and knocked his feet out from under him. This gave Sebastion time to get a jump on him in hopes of gaining an advantage over his opponent, but Deacon turned on him. The two moved in practiced form as they blocked or landed each attack. Each movement was fluid.

"I can't believe that Sebastion knows how to do this stuff." Rhonda watched him move fluidly around the yard. "I never would've guessed. He was always so quiet at work."

"His father was adamant that he be able to protect himself," Oscar explained. "Even if he didn't plan to be a hunter."

"He didn't want this life, did he?" Samantha asked.

"No." Oscar watched his nephew. "He wanted to go to school and get as far away from all this as he could."

"What happened that brought him into it?" Rhonda

asked.

"He is very smart." Oscar's eyes filled with pride. "He's good with computers and knows how to discreetly get information. Other hunters would come to him to find out things and get his help, and if you know Sebastion, you know he would do anything to help anyone." Oscar grew quiet. "We trained him and made sure he could fight and shoot, which he excelled at. When his parents were killed, he decided to become a hunter."

"That's so sad," Rhonda spoke softly.

"Many hunters have similar stories." Oscar stood up to stretch his legs.

"And what's your story?" Rhonda asked.

"My story is simple." He shrugged. "My father was a hunter and so was his father. I knew the evils of man and werewolf from the time I was a young boy, and I knew my job would be to protect both. I've been doing it ever since."

He strode over to where Deacon had Sebastion in a headlock. His face was turning red, but they were laughing despite the awkward angle he was bent over.

"Okay, that's enough." Deacon let go of him and stifled a laugh as he bent at the waist to catch his breath.

"Already?" Sebastion panted. "I had him right where I wanted him."

Deacon rolled his eyes as he pulled a couple bottles of water from a nearby cooler. He handed one to Sebastion, and the two of them quickly drank the whole bottle.

Oscar shook his head at them before motioning for the girls to join in. "Deacon, you pair with Samantha, and Rhonda, you'll be with Sebastion."

Samantha took her place in front of Deacon as he

gave a sly grin. She swallowed hard and took a deep breath. She hoped her body would remember the training that her mind had forgotten. Sooner rather than later. Every bird and creature of the woods grew silent. Even the breeze stopped.

"Whenever you're ready." Oscar waved for them to start.

She was ready even though she was perfectly fine with watching on the sidelines. They stepped around each other for a moment. He grabbed her hand and spun her around as if they were dancing instead of fighting. He pulled her to him and wrapped his arms around her waist with her back to him.

"I don't think we're practicing the right moves." She grinned.

"We're just warming up," he whispered in her ear, causing her face to heat.

She slipped from his grasp and rounded on him with a kick to his side, which he stopped with ease. He held her foot in his hands and wouldn't let it go. She managed to jump up with her other leg and land a kick to Deacon's chest, causing him to drop her foot. She caught herself before she hit the ground. She apologized, but he only smiled at her.

"I knew it would come back to you." He dusted off his shirt. His smile melted her. There was so much she wanted to do with him that didn't involve combat.

They continued their sparring match as Samantha remembered more moves that she couldn't believe she was able to pull off. As if she had done this every day of her life, she ran toward a tree and dug her foot into its hard bark, pushing herself into a backflip that landed her behind Deacon. She was hot and sweaty by the end of it, but she was having fun. She drank heavily from her water bottle as Sebastion and Rhonda caught her attention. He was trying to teach her to move her feet when she jumped on his back.

"You're not paying attention." Sebastion adjusted her weight so she wouldn't slide off.

"You lost me when you started explaining what a *kumite* was." Rhonda wrapped her slim arms around his neck and let him carry her over to the rest of the group.

He shook his head and stood up, letting her slide down onto her feet. "I don't know about you, but I'm starving." He patted his stomach.

"I'm on it." Rhonda jogged back into the cabin.

"How does she have that much energy?" Sebastion dropped on the picnic table.

"I've been asking her that for years." Samantha finished her water in one drink.

"Would you want to take a walk with me?" Deacon asked her. His face was childlike as he peered at her through his dark lashes.

"Where to?" Samantha asked.

"There's a trail just beyond those trees." Deacon pointed to an opening at the far end of the yard.

"Maybe I should stay and help Rhonda with the food," she said as she glanced back toward the cabin.

"We can manage the food." Oscar cleared the yard of all the training equipment as he spoke. "You kids have fun."

Samantha nodded to him and took Deacon's hand as he led her into the trees. "Should we be in here?" she asked Deacon as her eyes took a moment to adjust in the dim light of the woods.

"We're safe." He squeezed her hand in his. "No one

knows this cabin is here."

"Okay." Samantha spoke with more confidence than she felt. "Where are we going?" Two squirrels scurried up a large tree. The colors of this season were beautiful. The red and orange leaves stood out against the green pines and dark brown of the empty branches.

"There's something I want you to see." He led the way through the trail.

Rabbits ran from them as they approached. Leaves crumbled under their feet with each step. She could smell the earthy aroma of the dirt path as the breeze rustled through her ponytail. The farther into the woods they got, she heard a stream bubbling.

"Close your eyes." Deacon turned to face her.

She smiled and followed his request. He led her closer to the sound as sunshine warmed her face. The light stung her eyes as it glinted off the sparkling water. As she followed the stream, her eyes turned up to see a waterfall. "That's beautiful." Her words caught in her throat. It wasn't huge, but she had to raise her eyes up to see the very top of it.

"I come out here sometimes," Deacon confessed. "When I need to think or just have a moment of silence."

"It's a great spot," she said as she admired everything around her. The grass was lush around the water's edge.

Her eyes fell away from the waterfall and landed on him. He held her face in his hands, gently caressing her cheek with his thumb. They stood there for a long time before Deacon kissed her forehead and pulled her into his arms. She melted in his warm embrace as they held each other. The waterfall in the background and their beating hearts were the only sound.

"What are the odds that Sebastion will show up in the next five minutes?" Deacon pressed his head to hers.

"Knowing his record, I would say highly likely."

He pulled away from her with a laugh that sparked emotions inside of her.

"I love hearing you laugh," she confessed.

He smiled under her gaze. He backed away from her and removed his shirt. "Are you up for a swim?" He motioned his head toward the small pool of water below the waterfall.

His muscles rippled from the movement, and for a second, she forgot to breathe.

"It's probably freezing in there," Samantha said as she eyed the water to distract herself from the path her eyes were taking down his torso.

"I'll keep you warm." His fingers worked to unbuckle his belt. She forced herself not to follow the V pattern of his abs.

He jumped in the water, going under for a few seconds until breaking through the surface of the dark pool. His eyes were brighter while he was in the water.

"Are you coming in?" he asked her with a smile.

With some hesitation, she pulled off her top and leggings, feeling exposed but excited. With a deep breath, she crept to the edge of the clearing and plunged into the cool water. As she breached the surface and breathed in new air, the water had washed away all the sad things in her life. She expected it to be frigid, but it cooled her down enough to be comfortable.

Deacon pulled her to him and wrapped his arms around her waist. She was able to touch the bottom with the tips of her toes as they moved out of the pool's center.

"I've missed you. I thought I was hallucinating

when I saw you at that bakery, but there you were. After I woke up in your apartment, I wasn't sure if you'd remembered me."

She ran her hand through his hair as she remembered that night. "I didn't remember you at first, but there was something in your eyes that gave me hope. I couldn't let you die. I guess, deep down, I did remember."

"Do you remember your accident?" Deacon asked.

She placed a hand to his chest while she thought about it. "I remember rushing out of our house." She tried to sort through her memories. They were still scattered and were mostly feelings and flashes that ran across her mind. "Someone found where we were staying, so we had to get away. There was a car crash, and someone pulled me from the wreckage. I remembered my name when I woke up in the hospital as Samantha Walker, but now, I know we were going by Martin. We were in hiding."

"I didn't know. That's why I couldn't find you. I was searching for the wrong Samantha. I didn't mean to hurt you when I left. I thought it would keep you safe."

"My parents knew about the prophecy, and that's why we were in hiding." Her lip quivered as moisture built in her eyes. "I'm sorry I wasn't honest with you then. I was protecting you and your family. The less you knew, the better."

Deacon rested his forehead against hers. Even with his body heat to warm her, a chill ran up her spine, leaving her cold. "I shouldn't have brought it up."

"It's okay. It's sad, but I'm glad I can remember more now. Not knowing who I was before the accident really bothered me."

"I wish I could've given you happier memories."

197

"You are my happy memories." She held his face.

He caressed one hand as he held her tight in the other.

"Will you sing for me again?" She smiled.

"That was a one-time thing." Deacon tapped the tip of her nose with his index finger. A small drop of water dripped between them. "Well, maybe."

His eyes dropped to her lips as he held her close. She kissed his cheek and moved her lips to his neck. She kissed him slowly and softly until a low growl purred in his throat. He lifted her up slightly as she wrapped her legs around his waist. They stared deep into each other's eyes before he pressed his lips against hers.

Before the kiss deepened, he pulled away and strained his hearing, trying to tune in on any movement.

"What is it?" Samantha asked. The clearing was empty. She was expecting to see someone watching them, but there was nothing.

"I think that boy has given me PTSD."

"Who?" Samantha asked, not sure what he was talking about.

"Sebastion." Deacon shook water from his hair. "He's definitely the little brother I never had."

She busted out laughing and hugged him tightly around his neck.

"We should head back." Deacon placed a small kiss to her temple.

"Okay." She reluctantly agreed as he helped her out of the water.

The wind was chilly against her wet skin. They quickly slipped into their dry clothes and made their way back to the cabin. The closer they got, she could smell hamburgers cooking on the grill. Deacon's hand slid into hers as he brought it to his lips, kissing it gently. Her cheeks cramped from all the smiling, but she loved it, and she loved him. She wished they were still by the waterfall.

Oscar and Rhonda were tending to the grill as they stepped in the yard. Sebastion finished setting the picnic table with paper plates and plastic cutlery.

"I was just about to come after you two," Sebastion said over his shoulder as he tore off paper towels and folded them into neat squares. "The food's about done."

"Of course, you were," Deacon yelled back to him as he gave Samantha a sideways glance.

They both started laughing at the odd expression on Sebastion's face.

"What's so funny?" he asked.

"Nothing." Deacon's grin grew wide, revealing his beautiful teeth.

If there was one thing she could remember for the rest of her life, it was the happiness that only Deacon's laugh could bring. She smiled broadly at him as they neared the picnic table. She was on a vacation at last, and even though the circumstances weren't ideal, she couldn't help but feel happy. She had tasty food and great people around her. What more could a girl ask for?

Chapter 23

The weeks flew by since their first day of training, and she was feeling better than ever, but the blood moon would return soon. Her time was running out. Per Oscar's instruction, she was trying to tap into her abilities, but she couldn't access anything. Samantha hoped the first part of the procedure hadn't worked, but she knew that wasn't true. How else would she explain being able to heal like she could?

"Are you ready?" Deacon asked her as he held on to his Bo staff. It was a long wooden stick they were using to practice with as they remained hidden in their forest getaway. There had been no sign of Kiren and his pack or the hunters since arriving here. It was as if it all had been a bad dream.

She held tightly to her staff and nodded. They were practicing every day, and she was surprised at how quickly she caught on. Her family came from a line of strong and talented hunters that were thought to be the best in their field. She and Deacon approached each other and assumed their fighting positions. His suggestion to switch to short-range weapons so soon scared her. She was afraid she would do more damage to herself than her target, but she quickly grew to like it.

Deacon moved first. He was quick and agile, but he was holding back. He brought his staff down, and she blocked his advance easily. They went back and forth at a steady pace. Rhonda and Sebastion stopped their training to spectate. The sun was warm, but heavy clouds were filling the sky.

She spun around, causing her long hair to twirl as she ducked and dodged, blocking hit after hit. Her face was serious, but there was a hint of a smile on her lips. Deacon moved swiftly as he timed each move.

Sebastion rolled his eyes on the sidelines.

"You're holding back," Samantha acknowledged. They rounded on each other, waiting for the right moment to attack. Leaves crunched under each step, releasing their crisp aroma.

"Just a little." Deacon smiled.

"Don't." She jumped into the air and brought her staff down.

Her confidence showed through the slam of her weapon on his. She was stronger and faster than when they started training. This enticed and scared her. They didn't know what she was capable of yet. A dreadful thought crept into the back of her mind. What if training only made her a better killer?

Deacon blocked her attack and smoothly moved out of her way. He tapped her lightly on the butt with his staff jokingly. Rhonda and Sebastion giggled, but when she faced them, she wasn't laughing. Her face was deadly serious, and she narrowed her eyes.

"Again," she demanded as they closed in on each other.

Deacon stood at an angle from her before he sliced through the air with another attack. Samantha blocked him and seemed to move faster than before. Deacon barely missed her staff as she swung it down on him. She readied herself as the fight grew intense. It was less like practice and more like battle. Deacon matched her pace and used more of his strength to counter her attacks.

Neither of them were smiling anymore and were really getting into the duel. The air around them was charged as the sequence continued. Sebastion and Rhonda stood from their seat on the grass and backed away from them. Their expressions were serious and full of worry.

"We should stop them." Rhonda rubbed her hand over her mouth as she couldn't believe what she was seeing.

"I don't think that'd be a good idea." Sebastion linked his arm through hers and moved them closer to the cabin.

Oscar must have heard the commotion, as he came out to watch. The dead leaves in his yard started moving toward Samantha despite the lack of wind.

"Uh oh," he said as the fight brewed in front of him. He stepped back as he tasted static on his tongue.

"Samantha, this is supposed to be practice." Deacon barely avoided a hit to his face.

"You said I had to be prepared." She slid backward from the hard push from his staff. She stood firm on her feet. "This is me being prepared," she said as she twirled her staff around and set herself in a readied pose. "Stop holding back on me."

Deacon chanced a glance over to the house. An unnatural energy was coming from Samantha. They should stop, but she wasn't ready to quit as she lunged at him. He blocked her attack and swung his staff down at her as hard as he could. She blocked his swing, but the force snapped her stick in half.

She examined the broken pieces before glaring at

him. Anger darkened her hazel eyes as he slowly backed down. She reacted as if he'd broken her most prized possession. Samantha threw the sticks to the ground and advanced on him. He tossed his staff to the side and held his hands up in surrender.

"Samantha, that's enough," he asserted. "We should call it quits for now. I don't want to hurt you."

She smiled and readied herself to continue their duel in hand-to-hand combat.

"Don't make me do this." He pleaded with her, but she wasn't about to stop.

Samantha was moving just as fast as him as their colors blurred and melted together.

"Sebastion." Rhonda's eyes widened.

"Deacon won't hurt her," Sebastion said.

"She might hurt him," Oscar said as the fight continued. He eyed his gun cabinet through the kitchen window, that held his tranquilizers. He hoped it wouldn't come to that, but he had to be ready for anything.

The two moved so fast it was hard to keep up. Samantha landed a back kick to Deacon's chest, causing him to stumble and fall backward. He was off the ground just as fast as he landed as he prepared to end this. His eyes glowed brightly, and his canines grew slightly. He didn't want to hurt her, but she didn't seem to be in control anymore. This needed to stop before someone got hurt.

"You have to stop," Deacon yelled as he moved closer. An unnatural wind blew through his hair.

"Make me." Samantha positioned herself to attack again.

The two charged each other. He dodged the wide swing of her arm and grabbed her around the waist, locking her arms at her sides.

"Samantha." He tried to reason with her. "This isn't you. You have to stop."

"Let me go!" she yelled at him as she struggled to get free from his tight grip. She budged him slightly as her hands gripped his wrists.

Samantha's eyes shifted. They weren't glowing, but the color changed. Time slowed as leaves and debris rose from the ground around them.

"Let. Me. Go!" Samantha yelled as a force pushed out from her, sending leaves and sticks flying in every direction.

Sebastion, Rhonda, and Oscar took cover as Deacon was thrown by the invisible force. Samantha turned on him and focused on the pieces of her broken stick. The two halves hovered at her sides as if they had minds of their own. One of the halves soared toward Deacon and barely missed him. It would have punctured his heart.

He kicked off the ground and held up his palms in surrender. "Samantha, stop this. Don't do something you'll regret." The charge in the air around them pricked his skin as he breathed heavily. The other half of her stick floated next to her as she approached. Her features softened as she drew near. The stick dropped to the ground as she shook her head before meeting his eyes.

She swayed on her feet as the strength in her legs failed her, but Deacon was quickly at her side. He caught her before she hit the ground. He sat her down gently but didn't let her go.

"I'm sorry," she cried. "I couldn't stop myself."

"It's okay. You're okay." He smoothed his hand over her head as blood ran from her nose.

She wiped it away with her hand. The blood was

thick and black, and the sight of it sickened her. Fear filled her eyes.

"Let's get you inside," he said gently as he helped her stand.

Samantha stood and instantly regretted it. Her head spun, and her stomach twisted. The metallic tang of blood filled her mouth. Lightning flashed through the dark clouds, and thunder rumbled around them. She was having a tough time focusing on anything in front of her. The rain fell on them in heavy sheets as the clouds burst above them. The rain was cold, and it soaked through their clothes instantly.

"Come on." Deacon placed his hand against the small of her back and gently moved her forward. She stared frantically in front of her. She held out her hands as if to find her way through a darkened room.

"Samantha," Deacon said her name as he turned to Sebastion, Rhonda, and Oscar who were now on the porch, sheltered from the rain. "The steps are right in front of you."

"Where?" she asked, sounding panicked as she tried to find the banister with her hand. Its smooth wooden surface balanced her as she tried to position her foot onto the first step but stumbled. The jolt tightened her chest. She was breathing hard.

"Can't you see them?"

"Everything's blurry." She tried to move up the steps again on her own. Deacon tried to help, but she shook off his hands.

"I can walk up four steps!" she yelled. "I'm not a child." She cried as her outburst startled her. "I'm sorry." She shook her head and tried to blink away the blurriness. "I—"

Thunder boomed in the sky above them as the rain fell harder.

"Ah!" Samantha groaned as she held her head.

"What's wrong?" Deacon scanned her with worried eyes and listened to her irregular heartbeat.

"My head," she groaned. Her eyes were squeezed together in pain. "It's splitting open."

He pushed her hair out of her face. More blood ran from her nose. "Let's get you inside." Fear laced around each word.

Her surroundings spun before her. Her legs gave out as she fell into Deacon's arms. Her darkened blood leaked from one of her ears.

"Deacon," Samantha moaned. "What's happening to me?"

She passed out before he could respond. He pleaded to Oscar with his eyes, but they had run out of time. All they could do was keep her comfortable. She was going to die if they couldn't find a way to help her. His insides burned at the thought of losing her again. He picked her up and took her inside the cabin.

As he laid her down gently on the guest bed, he wiped away the blood from her nose and ears with the towel Rhonda handed him. He couldn't fight his way out of this situation. His face was blank as he shuttered.

"I'm sorry, Deacon," Oscar said to him. "I truly am."

He breathed heavily as his eyes glowed. Samantha was so still it was as if she was already gone. There had to be something he could do. There was one last choice he could think of, but he couldn't bring himself to say it aloud. If they finished the procedure, she would live, but he would still lose her. Either way, she was going to die, and if she did, he would take out anyone that stood between him and Michael.

Samantha couldn't open her eyes or move, but she was still aware of her surroundings. They were talking somewhere in the cabin. They tried every angle to save her, but it was hopeless. There was only one way she was going to survive. They couldn't bring her to Michael without being captured or worse. She thought of how much she loved them. She grew to like Oscar in the little time she'd known him, and if there was a way to save her, he would've found it.

She heard them leave as silence filled the cabin. She thought she was alone, until the bed dipped at her side, and Deacon's warm body moved closer to hers. His musky scent washed over her as he pulled the covers up around her shivering body. She managed to turn her face to him and slowly opened her eyes. He was blurry for a moment, but as she blinked, his face became clear. His hair was wet from the rain, as two drops of water slipped from the dark strands.

"Do you need anything?" he asked as he examined her face. She was pale, and dark veins appeared through her skin. Her beautiful hazel eyes lost some of their usual brightness. He tucked a loose strand of hair behind one ear. Her hot skin heated the back of his hand before he returned her gaze. *This can't be happening.*

"I have all I need right here." She smiled, but her lips no longer had their rosy hue. "I'm sorry for before." Her frail voice threatened to shatter his heart. "I don't know what came over me."

"It's okay." He spoke gently. "You got lucky on that last hit. Next time I won't go easy on you."

Next time. This made her laugh despite everything.

The smile faded from her face as she spoke again. "I don't think there will be a next time."

"Don't say that. You're going to be fine," he said in a tight voice. His brows furrowed together. She knew his anger was a way to hold back the sadness she saw in his eyes.

"Deacon, I need you to promise me something." She gritted her teeth together as she sat up to face him.

"Anything." He held her waist and moved to hold her close. The old bed creaked under his weight.

"If anything happens to me—" She coughed. "—promise me you'll leave Glenwood and not go after Michael."

He averted his eyes. She put a gentle hand on his face and turned him so she could see him. He kept his eyes turned downward but slowly brought them up to meet her gaze.

"I'm serious. I need you to promise me you'll get out and take Sebastion and Rhonda with you. I don't want them or you to get hurt."

He dropped his gaze to her lips and lingered there. "I promise."

She hoped he would keep his promise, because what she was about to do was going to change everything. She would never kill anyone no matter what kind of control Michael thought he would have over her. Especially Deacon. She loved him, and love would be enough. If she couldn't stop herself, she hoped they would get as far away from her as possible so she couldn't hurt them if she were wrong.

She knew there were other hunters out there. Good ones. She thought of Oscar then. He would find a way. If there was another choice, it was out of their reach.

Time was not on their side, and she didn't want to die. Not yet.

Deacon held her soft face in his hands. Sadness turned to anger in his tight chest. He had the most beautiful and amazing woman in front of him, but he was about to lose her. There was nothing else he could do but to stay with her. He slowly brought his lips to hers and kissed her gently. He could taste her blood in his mouth as their kiss grew deeper. He gently laid her back onto the bed as she pulled him tightly against her body.

She peered into his shimmering eyes as they glowed softly. He was beautiful and was the most caring man she had ever met. Leaving him was going to be the hardest thing she would ever do. His chest moved in time with her breathing. She saw perfect white teeth behind his parted lips.

"I love you," she whispered.

He bent over her as he ran his hands over her arms, pushing them tenderly above her head. He slid his hands under her wet shirt and held her waist as he brushed his lips against hers again before he spoke. "I've always loved you," he whispered in her ear as he kissed her neck. "I never stopped loving you."

The breath from his whispered words shot heat through her body as she shivered from the fever. She held him tightly to her and wished she had more time. There was a lot she hadn't seen and done. She couldn't bear to watch their faces as she slowly died in front of them. The decision was set in her mind, and as soon as she had the opportunity, she would put her plan into motion.

Samantha pushed thoughts of death from her mind as she opened herself up fully to Deacon. She would always love him. She would hold on to this feeling of being with him for as long as she could, and she knew that would be how she would win. She would not let Michael destroy what they had. With every fiber of her being, she would protect them like they have protected her. Evil would not win. Not this time.

Chapter 24

Sebastion pushed air sorrowfully from his lungs as Rhonda stared at the cabin door. His shoulders slumped in defeat. They shivered from the cold wind that stirred the rain onto the covered porch. There had to have been something more they could've done. He read all the books and researched ancient texts, but there was nothing to find. *This can't be the end.*

"Sebastion," Oscar shouted from inside the car. He called him over with a nod of his head, but he was frozen in place. His uncle's eyes glistened with their failure. With all his knowledge and smarts, Sebastion had no answers. No solution. There was no magic pill or incantation that would save Samantha.

Rhonda was the first one out of the cabin when Oscar suggested a supply run, but she hadn't moved an inch since the door slammed closed behind them. Her pink tank top hugged her shoulders with each shuddering breath.

"Rhonda," Sebastion whispered as he gently slid his hand across the small of her back. He stood in front of her when she didn't respond. "Rhonda," he repeated. "We'll be back soon. Deacon needs to say goodbye to—"

"None of us should be saying goodbye to her!" she snapped as tears streamed down her tanned cheeks. "Not now. Not so soon." She glanced at the door before glaring up at him.

"I'm so sorry." Sebastion's voice cracked.

"You're not the one who needs to be sorry." She gritted through her teeth. "Michael is."

He searched her eyes. Her lips snarled as his name left her mouth.

"He'll get what's coming to him." Sebastion's skin burned with hatred.

"She's my sister," Rhonda moaned. "I can't—" She covered her face with her hands and leaned into Sebastion's chest. Her sobs wrecked him as he held her tightly.

"We...I'll fix this." He stammered. "There has to be a way." A vision of his mother's body surfaced in his mind. Her auburn eyes haunted him. That night would be with him always. He failed to save her and his father just as he was failing now.

"You heard Oscar." Rhonda pulled back from him to wipe her eyes. "We're out of time."

"We have until the blood moon ends," he corrected as he caught a final tear that slipped from her eye with his thumb. "Plenty of time for a miracle."

"We need a miracle right now." Rhonda smiled sadly.

"Good thing miracles are my specialty." He tugged gently on the two long braids that fell over her chest. "Let's go get snacks. The more sugar, the better." Her smile soothed a fracture in his heart. *This isn't the end.* They hustled to the car where Oscar was waiting on them. His hand went to the cross necklace around his neck. The back was worn smooth from wear.

There was a break in the rain as they arrived at the outlet store. The clouds parted enough for the sun to warm them. Sebastion was deciding between chocolate or powdered donuts when he noticed Eli in one of the nearby aisles. It was odd finding him so far out of town.

"Sebastion?" Eli said, attempting to sound surprised. "What brings you out this way?" he asked as he stepped into their aisle. His green eyes took in Rhonda before moving back to him. "Who's this?"

"This is Rhonda. We work together at the hospital. Rhonda, this is Eli." Sebastion introduced them.

"Nice to meet you," Eli said with hungry eyes. "Haven't seen you in a while. Where've you been, and what happened to your face? Did you go a few rounds with Mike Tyson or what?"

"Eh. It was an accident. I've been visiting family." He slid his hands into his jean's pockets. "I took some time off work."

"How is good old Oscar these days?" Eli leaned on the shelf next to him.

Sebastion eyed him as he realized he couldn't recall ever telling him about his uncle. "He's fine," he said as he tried to remain calm. "What brings you out this way?"

"Just riding around." Eli picked at one of his fingernails. "Thought I'd stop for some food."

Sebastion nodded and glanced behind Eli to see his uncle. His stomach twisted in knots as a chill ran down his spine. They needed to leave. "Rhonda," he said, turning his attention to her. "Could you take this stuff to the front for me? I'll meet you in the car."

She eyed him with confusion before casting a sideways glance at Eli. "Yea." She hesitated. "Of course." She smiled at them and walked over to Oscar. They exchanged words before peering at him around Eli's tall frame. The cashier busied himself as he scanned and bagged their items. Each beep of his scanner raised his pulse. He turned his focus to Eli when they were safe back in the car.

"Why'd you have to do that?" Eli asked.

"Do what?" Sebastion answered his question with one of his own.

"I guess she's calling Deacon?" Eli asked as Rhonda placed her cell phone to her ear. They had an unobstructed view of them through the store windows. She paced nervously. The glint in his eyes unnerved him. "I didn't see him with you when you came in. Is he with his precious Samantha?"

"How do you know about them?" Sebastion was surprised to hear those names leave his mouth.

"Oh, I know about a lot. Kiren sends his regards." Eli's eyes glowed an eerie green as he flashed his fangs.

Sebastion stepped back a little too fast as pain stabbed through his side. His ribs were healing, but if he moved too fast or breathed in too deeply, they ached.

"Someone beat you up pretty good, didn't they?" Eli leaned in closer. The leather of his jacket mixed with a musky smell that reminded him of a basement.

"It's not been my week," Sebastion muttered as he surveyed the small store. There was just one other customer inside aside from the clerk. He hoped there were enough witnesses to keep Eli from doing anything rash.

"It's about to get a whole lot worse if you don't tell me what I need to know." Eli spoke as he bared his teeth.

"I don't know where they are. We split up," Sebastion lied. "And if I did, I wouldn't tell you."

"Oh, I think you would," Eli said as he returned his green eyes back to the window. "I'd hate for anything to happen to your girl. I have her scent, so you know I could find her anywhere. She's a treasure."

Sebastion followed his gaze. "You won't touch her."

"I've been shopping for a new mate. I think she'd be perfect," he said, turning away from the window to glare at him. He rolled his neck and smirked.

"This whole time you've been pretending to be my friend, and for what?" Sebastion's anger started to boil over. "To get to Deacon? You're no match for him, and you know it."

Eli slammed him against one of the coolers behind him and held him in place with a clawed hand. "It's not just me he has to worry about." Eli pierced his skin with his claws. "Kiren's pack has grown since he last dealt with Deacon, and now, I'm second-in-command."

Sebastion gritted his teeth and glared into his ghoulish eyes. He ignored the pain in his shoulder as he spoke. "Why are you doing this? You know what Kiren's capable of. Why follow him?"

"I don't want any trouble in here, boys," the man behind the counter yelled back to them, interrupting Sebastion. "Make your purchases and hit the road before I call the cops."

"We were just leaving," Eli said politely to the man as he retracted his claws. "You first?" He motioned for Sebastion to take the lead.

Sebastion moved around Eli but didn't turn his back to him. He kept him in his sights as they left the store. The bright sunlight hurt his eyes, but he continued to watch every step Eli took. There were no other businesses in the area, so they were very much alone.

Eli sauntered out into the open. His whole demeanor changed from the person Sebastion thought he knew.

"That's far enough." Oscar raised his pistol at him. "Sebastion, get in the car. Now."

"We were just having a little conversation, Unc." Eli closed the distance between them.

"I said that's far enough," Oscar repeated as he cocked the pistol.

"Think you can get a shot off before I rip your throat out, old man?" Eli antagonized him.

"Why don't you try it and see?" Oscar retorted, keeping the gun leveled at Eli's chest.

Sebastion dug out another pistol from the car. He was banged up, but he could still shoot. He hoped they were out of sight enough from the clerk so he wouldn't call the police on them. As the men stood on the dirt and gravel that made up the store's small parking area, the familiar roar of Deacon's motorcycle grew louder in the distance.

"Backup is on the way." Eli grinned as the motorcycle came into view. "That just leaves one question." He turned back to face Oscar and Sebastion. "Who's left to guard Samantha?"

They glanced at each other as they realized what they had done. They lowered their weapons and searched the area, but Eli was nowhere to be found.

"He can't know where the cabin is." Oscar tried to assure Sebastion. "There's no way."

"You heard him, Oscar." Sebastion put his hands on the hood of the car. The metal was warm against his clammy skin. Rhonda got out and joined them as Deacon pulled in. He parked the bike and jogged over to them.

"What's going on?" Deacon asked them.

"We have a problem. Remember when I told you about Eli? Well, he's with Kiren."

"I caught the werewolf's scent as soon as I rolled in. What'd he want?"

"Forget him. We have to get back to the cabin," Rhonda urged Deacon before anyone answered his questions. "Kiren's pack know where she is."

"I just passed a black SUV on my way over here." He growled and jumped on his bike as the others got in the car and peeled out, throwing gravel everywhere. The car swerved as it matched the bike's pace.

"He's going to wreck that thing." Rhonda gasped. He took the curves way over the speed limit.

"He knows what he's doing. I doubt this pack knows the location of my cabin. We could be leading them back there now. This could be a setup." Oscar's eyes were narrowed as he struggled to keep the car on the wet road.

"We can't risk it. If they're following us, we'll deal with them then." Sebastion's voice was calm, but his eyes never left the road. "He'll kill her."

They pulled into the driveway that led to the cabin. Deacon's bike was parked, but he wasn't on it.

"My car's gone," Rhonda mentioned when they got out of the car.

"Why would they take your car?"

"They didn't," Deacon said as he walked out of the cabin, holding a slip of paper in his hand. The sky was growing increasingly dark as the sun dropped lower in the sky. The blood moon could be seen in the distance. "She's gone, but no one took her. She left." He jogged down the steps with his head hung low.

"She left? Where did she go?" Rhonda stammered.

"She wrote this note." Deacon ran his hand over Samantha's soft handwriting. "She went to Michael to complete the prophecy."

"What? No, she wouldn't do that," she said as tears formed in her eyes. "That's…no."

"I should've known," Deacon said.

"You couldn't have known she would make this choice." Oscar slid his pistol into his shoulder holster.

"She made me promise that no matter what happened to her I wouldn't go after Michael." His muscles twitched as he paced on the gravel driveway. "She wanted me to leave Glenwood with all of you."

"Can I read the note, please?" Rhonda asked. He handed it to her. With a shaky voice, she read it aloud.

I'm sorry to run off this way, but there was no other choice. I couldn't bear to let all of you watch me die. I know you did all you could to figure this out, and I appreciate it more than you'll ever know. Please don't be mad at me. This is no one's fault but my own. I got you all into this, and now I'm going to end it. My love for you all will be my weapon to fight Michael's control, but if I should lose this battle, I know Oscar and his team can take me out.

Deacon, please keep your promise. Don't come after me!

Tears streamed down her face.

Sebastion wrapped his arms around her as he read the rest of the letter to himself. "We can't let her do this." He crushed the letter in his fist.

"Deacon," Oscar said as he moved to his side. "When you left the warehouse, you destroyed the machine, right? Could they have repaired it?"

"I knocked it over, and sparks flew from it. We didn't have a lot of time. They could have fixed it by now. I don't know."

"If she can fight his control, this may work out to

our advantage." Oscar squeezed his shoulder. "I can gather my team and maybe a few more if I can persuade them to join us. We'll need time and a distraction."

"I have an idea," Deacon suggested.

"No way," Sebastion interrupted. "That's just what they want. They will make her kill you. You're a part of the prophecy too." His face flamed red as he wracked his brain for a better way. The smell of blood and flowers mixing with the musty smell of that room came to him as he recalled that night.

"She won't kill me." Deacon locked eyes with him. "I know she won't."

"I don't like it," he said. "It's too risky."

"We have to try." Oscar eyed his nephew. "How long do you need?"

"One hour." Oscar scratched the stubble on his chin. "Two at the most."

Deacon nodded as thunder clapped in the distance. The sky was black in the direction toward the warehouse. A new storm was approaching. Samantha was right about one thing. This would all end tonight, and they hoped it would end in their favor. They couldn't lose her to Michael. The rain fell on them in heavy sheets. This couldn't be the end. Not like this.

Chapter 25

Eli stood hidden in the trees that lined the road leading to the warehouse. Rain soaked his clothes as his night vision focused on Samantha. He didn't expect she would go back to the hunters on her own, but there she was, trudging up the path from the crumbling remains of the old school. They followed her to this place. He rolled his eyes at the sound of her heavy breathing.

"Pathetic. Are you sure about this?" he spoke toward the shadows.

"Are you questioning me, Eli?" Kiren turned his ghostly yellow eyes on him. His deep voice made him bow his head as he stepped into the moonlight.

"No," Eli responded, not meeting his eyes. "If they finish the ritual, she could kill us all. I want to be sure nothing will happen to you if you try to change her."

"It will work." Kiren flashed his fangs at his beta. "We may lose some to the hunters, but in the end, it will have been worth it."

He ran his hands through his soaking wet hair and wiped the rain from his eyes. They were more than eager to shed some hunter blood as a means to an end.

Kiren lifted his chin as he glared down his nose at the warehouse. "The McCrays have been a pain in my side for years. They don't deserve to have her."

"What if she rebels against you like Deacon did?" Eli braved a side-glance at his master. "What if she won't submit?"

Kiren flashed his eyes. A low growl emanated from deep within him as he stalked toward him. "Do you doubt your leader?"

"No." Power rolled in waves off Kiren as he shadowed him. "Of course not."

"Good. Is everyone in place?"

"They're all set," Eli spoke as he glanced into the forest behind them. Eyes glowed from every angle in the shadows.

He didn't understand why Kiren needed so many in his pack for this mission, but he knew better than to question him. They had more numbers than before. Many of them were fellow betas to Kiren before he became alpha of his own pack. They were just as dark and infinitely more bloodthirsty. *This plan will work after all.*

Kiren neared the edge of the cliff they were using as their vantage point. With the toe of his boot, he kicked a pebble over the side and flashed a hungry smile to the pack. "Let's raise a little hell, shall we?"

****

Samantha shivered from the freezing rain. She still had a fever, and her muscles tensed with every cool breeze. The large entrance doors of the warehouse loomed over her as she stared at them for a long time. She took a deep breath to calm herself as she raised her hands up to the heavy doors. She closed her eyes and reached into herself for that familiar pull. She let power flow from within her and released it from her hands, causing the doors to swing open with a loud crash. She wanted everyone inside to hear her.

The smell of sawdust and motor oil rolled out of the

entryway. Before she was ten feet inside, she was stopped. A group of men approached, attempting to grab her arms, but she sent them flying away from her with a push of her mind. She was here of her own accord and would not be handled like a prisoner. The men repositioned themselves, aiming their weapons at her. Some glanced to the man next to them as if waiting for orders.

"Where is he?" she shouted. Each word was edged with hate. Her eyes connected with every man in that room.

"I'm right here." Michael maneuvered through the group in front of her. "Have you come to take us all on? Aww, what's wrong? Feeling a little rough tonight?" He smiled smugly at her.

"I came here to finish this." Every fiber of her being wanted to kill everyone here, but there had been too much killing already. No one would die by her hands. Not tonight. Not ever. Something inside of her wanted to finish the ritual for a darker purpose, and the thought scared her.

"Smart girl," he sneered. "This way."

A couple of men approached her, and she stared them down until they backed away.

"Leave her be." Michael ushered them away with a wave of his hand.

He led her back to the procedure room. Light glinted off the exam table sitting next to the machine, causing her courage to falter, but she clenched her teeth and forced herself to move forward. The doctor was leaning on his palms behind the table. The lingering bruise on his cheek where Sebastion punched him was now green and yellow.

"We're cutting this too close." The doctor huffed at Michael. His jaws jiggled from the tightness in his voice.

"We have time."

The doctor nodded and gestured for Samantha to take her place. "When you're ready, my dear."

The icy steel of the table stung the backs of her legs as she forced herself to lay down. Her back ached as if she had been hit by a car. She focused on the ceiling as she tried controlling her breathing. The doctor and Michael strapped her arms and legs to the table once again. The leather burned and pinched her skin as they pulled them tighter.

"This will not be pleasant for you, but it will be over rather quickly." The doctor squeezed her arm. Her skin crawled under the clammy touch of his palm.

Michael stepped away from the bed as the doctor prepared the last part of the ritual. Above her, the ceiling parted, revealing the blood moon. Cold rain dropped onto her body as the crimson light of the moon shone down on her. She disconnected herself from the pain of the small needle pricks on her body. The doctor worked quickly assembling the tubing.

Switches and knobs clicked and hummed on the machine as they were turned on. A sob escaped her lips as she jumped. Heat grew closer until it touched her skin. Her veins were on fire. The molten silver coursed through the tubes and into her body until the vat ran dry. Her hands clenched into fists as she returned her gaze to the blood moon above her.

Sweat beaded and slipped off her body as pressure built in her chest. Even the tears that filled her eyes were hot. The restraints tightened the more she pulled at them as the pain became unbearable. She wished she would have gone off on her own and died rather than try to survive this. Samantha closed her eyes tightly. The dark entity building inside of her welcomed the transformation. The dark force seeped into every bone and curled its way into each muscle and tendon with a smile.

If she was going to end this, she had to be strong enough to do so. This was the only way. The pain was more than she could bear, as she thought her heart would explode. The force coming from the blood moon was like a weighted blanket as the effect helped her body to accept the silver. Her skull was close to cracking as her thoughts raced. In that moment, a smiling face appeared in her mind.

"I love you!" the woman's voice said in her head.

Samantha couldn't believe what she was seeing. She recognized the face. It was her mother! Tears spilled from her eyes as she smiled back.

Her mother spoke to her as if they were far away from this place. "Men will hunt you for what they think you can be for them," her mother's voice echoed. "But you are stronger than anything they can do to you."

Samantha wanted to hug her mother as she remembered flashes of their lives together. "Mom." Tears ran down Samantha's face.

"It's okay," her mother's voice said. "I love you."

The flashes of memories melted away, and she was back in the warehouse again. She glared at the moon as if it betrayed her. She was forever changed. With a scream that shook the very foundation of the building, sparks flew from the machine as it caught fire. Lights flickered, and the men gathered around them gasped. The ritual was complete.

****

Deacon raced down the narrow road on his motorcycle when Samantha's scream echoed around him. Before he could slow down his bike, something forced him off the road. He tumbled from the bike onto sharp gravel that dug into his side as he slid off the path leading to the warehouse. He got to his feet and moved toward the entrance. His breath fogged the air in front of his face.

The metal doors were warped as if an explosion busted through them. They barely hung on their hinges. As he walked into the building, his hatred for this place boiled his blood. The all-too-familiar click of guns being cocked caught his attention as their sights trained on him. He slowly raised his hands, showing he wasn't going to fight.

The men moved in, taking extreme caution. He recognized a few of them from their last encounter. They snarled and glared at him through bruised eyes as if he were a rabid dog that needed to be put down. In their minds, that's exactly what he was.

"Where is she?" he demanded.

"You'll see soon enough." One of the men struck him on the back of the head with the butt of his rifle. His body barely registered physical pain as the pain in his heart threatened to consume him. He fell to one knee and kept his eyes on the floor as another man tied his wrists behind his back.

"Get up." The man urged him as he tugged on the back of his T-shirt.

The men led him to the open room he found Samantha in before, but this time she was nowhere to be seen. He spotted Michael standing next to the doctor. He had a smile stretched across his arrogant face. He enjoyed seeing him with his hands bound.

"You really are making this easy for me, aren't you?" Michael asked him as he moved away from the exam table.

"Where is she?"

"Oh, don't worry. You'll see her soon enough." Michael motioned to the man standing closest to Deacon. "Release him." Michael picked a piece of lint from his sleeve as the man hesitated. "Now."

He nodded and did as Michael asked. Deacon pulled his arms in front of him, rubbing the soreness from his wrists. His sideways glare had the man backing away. The smell of fear permeated the room. The scent turned his stomach, but he was glad he hadn't completely lost his edge. He returned his sights to Michael as he realized love made him stronger, not weaker.

"On your knees," Michael ordered as he took a final bite out of an apple he was holding before tossing it to the side. He flicked his eyes to another man standing behind Deacon when he didn't do as he ordered. The man hit him hard enough to bring stars to his eyes and forced him to his knees. "See, I knew you could be trained." Michael spoke as if Deacon were nothing but a pet. "You have to have the right motivation."

"I want to see her," Deacon demanded. "Now." Blood ran down his neck from the hit behind his ear, but the wound was already stitching itself back together.

"As you wish." Michael's eyes flicked toward one of the side rooms. "Samantha. Come here, please." He held his hand out in the direction he spoke.

The door that led to a side room opened as his heart pounded in his chest to the rhythm of footsteps.

Samantha walked out from the shadows. She was no longer wearing her usual T-shirt and jeans, and she was no longer sick. She was wearing a black leather outfit with black combat boots. The outfit hugged her body like a second skin. The color had returned to her face and hair as it flowed behind her. She took Michael's hand.

The very air around them crackled at her appearance. Michael pulled her to him and kissed her deeply. Deacon turned his eyes to the floor, unable to bear the sight of them together. Samantha kissed him back. She pulled away from Michael and turned toward him. He didn't want to accept what he was seeing.

Her eyes were trained on the floor as she slowly brought them to meet his. The Samantha he knew was gone. Her eyes glowed unnaturally. The warm hazel irises were replaced by a color that wasn't purple but wasn't quite blue either. The flecks of silver in them added to the eerie sight. He clinched his fists at his side.

"No," he said to the room. "Samantha?" He called to her as he tried to get to his feet. One of the men hit him with a cattle prod sending volts of electricity through his body, causing him to drop to his hands and knees. She moved closer as his muscles were forced to contract. She placed a cool hand under his chin and gently pulled him to his knees. He wanted to touch her, but a strange energy came off her body in waves. He kept still as he searched her face for any sign of recognition, but there was nothing there.

Chapter 26

She stared blankly at the man before her, and she didn't know him, but what she did recognize was the scent that came from him. "Have you come here seeking your end, werewolf?" she asked him in a voice that no longer sounded like Samantha. She released his face and stepped back from him, putting a few inches between them.

"What?" Deacon couldn't believe what he was hearing. "Samantha, you know me."

"I only know your kind, and I know your kind must be destroyed. That is how it's always been."

Her words hit him like a fist to his gut as all the air left his lungs. He had to make her remember. It was their only chance. "Don't you remember? We were together. You, me, Sebastion, and Rhonda. Do you not remember them?"

"If they are like you, then they will get their turn to leave this world with Death. If it is their destiny." Hearing those words come from her gave him an idea.

"The Samantha I knew didn't believe in destiny," Deacon retorted. "She believed we made our own paths, and she didn't believe in killing. She believed in love."

Samantha cast her eyes down on him as they continued to glow. "Then she is a fool and is weak. I am not her." Her features darkened as she raised her chin.

"She's magnificent, isn't she?" Michael asked as he

walked up to face Deacon. He bent down and tightened his hand around his throat. "And she's all mine." He smiled wickedly at him.

Michael stood and swung his fist hard at Deacon's face, connecting with his cheekbone. Blood ran down his cheek as he supported his weight on one hand. He glared at Michael as he walked away from him. His fangs pushed against his restraint as his claws begged for release. He could end him now, but Oscar needed time to get everyone in place.

"It's time," Michael said to Samantha. "Kill him," he ordered as he rubbed the knuckles on his hand.

Her lips turned upward into a deadly smile. She placed her hand gently to his injured face and used her thumb to wipe away the streak of blood that ran from the wound. "It is time." Her otherworldly voice chilled him to the bone. She placed her free hand on his shoulder and closed her eyes.

Without thinking, he stood and quickly kissed her. He pulled her to his body and let his love for her move through his lips onto hers. The air in his lungs was thick with floral haze that flowed from her. The wooziness in his head begged for fresh air, but he held her tighter. She pulled away and glared at him. For a moment, the glow in her eyes dimmed, and her hazel eyes showed through for a split second. "Samantha," he said breathlessly, "I love you. I will always love you." His throat was closing as each word croaked out.

"Kill him!" Michael screamed. "Kill him now!"

Samantha faced him, and for a hopeful second, he thought he got through to her, but her eyes returned to their glowing form, unfazed by his confession.

"I do not love you." She placed one hand on his

shoulder and the other on his chest.

She closed her eyes in concentration, and when she reopened them, her power hit him and enveloped his body. His eyes glowed a bright blue as she forced him into the change. His fangs and claws grew with each wave that hit him. He could taste blood in his mouth. He recognized the familiar sting of silver and the floral scent of aconite as pain began to rack his body.

She held him in her hands as he finished transforming into his werewolf form. His beating heart pumped heavily under her palm as he dropped to his knees. She knelt in front of him to stay connected with his body. She didn't need to touch him to use her powers on him, but something about his touch was familiar, and she couldn't resist it. She pushed away the thought and slammed another wave of her power down on him.

"Samantha," he choked. "Don't do this. This isn't who you are."

He raised his shaking hands up to touch hers and wrapped them gently around her wrists. The beat of her heart shifted when their eyes met.

"We were friends," Deacon said as the thick floral scent of wolfsbane came from her and filled his lungs, weakening him. "We saved each other." The essence of silver worked its way through his veins as if he had been shot again by a silver bullet. "You made me promise not to come here after you, but I broke that promise. I broke a lot of promises I made to you, and I'm sorry."

"Be quiet, dog!" Samantha growled as her concentration broke.

There was less pressure coming from her as he put all the energy he had left into his legs, forcing himself to stand.

"Finish him!" Michael yelled from somewhere behind Samantha. Deacon's eyelids became heavy as his body shut down.

"You said you wouldn't let him control you," Deacon whispered to her as the room grew dark. His voice sounded as if he were talking in a tunnel. He was running out of time. He was going to die. "Don't let him control you. You don't have to be his weapon," Deacon managed to say between rigid breaths. "Remember me." He kissed her one last time.

The longer Deacon held his lips to Samantha's, the slower his heart pumped. He pulled away from her as his lungs contracted, keeping him from taking in air. He fell onto his back as he writhed in pain. Death's icy hand tightened around his throat as the silver snaked its way to his heart. Each time he blinked his eyes, it was a struggle to reopen them as everything moved in slow motion.

She withdrew her power from his body as he struggled to hold on. The sight of him writhing on the floor tugged at her heart. He meant nothing to her. *Was he just another beast to be executed, or was he something more?* She stepped away from Deacon. She had to stop. She needed to save him.

Sharp pains shot through her and ran down the nerves in her arms until her hands tingled. She held her head in her hands as she swayed on her feet. Something inside her was fighting to gain control.

"Samantha," Michael said behind her. She slowly turned to face him. "I command you to finish him. Now!" He yelled, causing spit to shoot from his mouth as he glared at her. His face twisted into anger as if he was the rabid animal.

Deacon arched his back as his face twisted with agony. With his last breath, his clenched fists relaxed. He was no longer moving, as if he were sleeping. One of the men kneeled to his side and checked his pulse at his neck.

"He, he has no pulse, sir," the man stammered before returning to his place with the others.

Part of her knew this was what was supposed to happen, but something deep inside herself screamed and cursed her for what she did.

"Perfect," Michael said as he moved to Samantha's side. "You did good. I can't wait to use you in the field." He smiled at her as he held her face in his hands. He pushed his lips hard against hers. His touch sickened her.

She pushed him away, breaking their kiss. "Use me?"

"Yes," he said plainly. "You are my weapon, and together, no one will stand in my way."

Her pulse quickened as her breathing picked up. She held her hand to her temple as a battle raged within her. Her muscles tightened as adrenaline flooded her system. "Who are you to think you can use me?" she spat at him in a voice she didn't recognize.

"You have no choice." His smile formed into a sneer. "I own you now." He put his hand to her throat.

"Sir!" one of the men shouted. From the ground, Deacon coughed as he drew in a deep raspy breath. The blue of his eyes glowed. "He's alive!"

Deacon leaned his weight on one arm as he pushed himself into a raised position. He stumbled at first when he tried to stand and dropped to one knee, but he was alive, if only just barely. Dark blood ran from his nose as he shook his head.

"How can this be? Finish him!" Michael spat into

Samantha's face as he kicked Deacon in the chest, knocking him down.

His chest was hardly moving as his head lolled to the side. He was strong, but another hit from her power, and he would never move again. Her eyes heated as their glow burned brightly. "I can't!" Samantha said as she held herself back from accessing her powers. The entity clawed at the cage she stuffed it into in her mind.

"I order you to kill him!" Michael yelled again.

Her soul was splitting in half as she lowered her eyes to the ground.

"Fine," Michael said through gritted teeth. "I'll do it myself."

Michael pulled his gun from his shoulder holster and took aim at Deacon. His silver bullets would be enough to kill him now in his weakened state if he shot him in the heart.

A calm enveloped her as she managed to bury the entity deep within herself. It fought and clawed at her nerves, but she held strong. She faced Michael, putting herself between them just as he fired the gun. One bullet lodged deep in her hip, but she could no longer feel physical pain.

The bullet pushed its way out of her and pinged off the hard floor. The wound instantly healed, leaving nothing more than a tear in her outfit.

"Don't. Touch him," Samantha growled at Michael. Tears stung her eyes as her anger exploded.

Michael was no longer in control of his weapon. "Kill them," he ordered his men. "Kill them both."

Rifles were raised and clicked into firing positions as they took aim at them. She tapped into her powers, and as the bullets raced toward them, she was able to stop each round in midair. The men were shocked by this even after all they witnessed here. Some backed away but not soon enough. She pushed hard with her mind, sending most of them sailing through the air. Some slammed against walls while others toppled over the men behind them.

She swayed slightly on her feet from the dizziness. Using her powers without the entity was strenuous. She turned around in time to see Michael aim his gun at her head. Before he could pull the trigger, Deacon was between them. He grabbed Michael's wrist and thrust the gun toward the ceiling as he roared into his face, causing fear to appear in Michael's eyes. He bent his wrist until he dropped his weapon, and he threw him onto the exam table and machinery. A loud explosion within the building shook the very ground they were standing on.

Deacon pulled Samantha to him. "Are you..." His eyes were unfocused as he wiped blood from his lip. "Are you okay?"

"I'm okay," she said with tears in her eyes. "I'm so sorry. I thought I killed you. I couldn't stop it."

"You came close." Deacon smiled slightly before pressing his lips tightly to hers.

She laughed and cried at the same time, but the moment was cut short as everything erupted around them. Glass from the high windows around the room burst as men rushed in through every exit. Samantha noticed Sebastion at Oscar's side as they fought and disarmed some of the remaining men from Michael's team, but what concerned her the most was seeing Kiren walk through one of the holes that had been blasted through the back wall. Flames licked his jeans as he casually strolled through the opening. He had a deadly smile on his face, and he was focused on her.

"Samantha, you have to get out of here," Deacon rushed.

"I'm not leaving. I can help."

Chaos was taking place before them. He searched her eyes and nodded but had a worried expression on his face. She was right, but he would feel better if she was far away from this place.

Chapter 27

They parted from each other to help Oscar's team fight off the werewolf pack along with Michael's men. They were in for a fight, and death was a hungry beast.

Samantha's muscles were strong and aching for her to put them to use. She pushed out with her mind and ripped the weapons from the hands of Michael's men that were bearing down on Oscar. It was easy to tell each group apart despite the chaos. All of Michael's men were outfitted in the same tactical gear, while Oscar's team were dressed in plain clothes. The wolves stood out with their glowing eyes, and Samantha gasped at how many there were.

She spotted Sebastion just as he flipped one of the men over his back and landed a heavy punch to his face. Creeping up behind him was one of the werewolves. This wolf had green glowing eyes that were filled with bloodlust. His lips spread into a wide grin as saliva dripped from his fangs.

"Sebastion!" she yelled as she started to run to his aid but was halted by something sharp as it penetrated her back. She grunted as the hot steel slid inside her, tearing and separating her skin and muscle.

"If I can't have you." Michael spoke in her ear over all the noise around them as he pushed the blade deeper into her back. "Then no one will."

She met Deacon's eyes as true fear spread across his face. He had transformed like the others but was no longer paying attention to the fighters around him. He launched into a sprint toward her but was caught by Kiren. He ripped through Deacon's shirt, tearing flesh along with fabric. They roared at each other with bared fangs and claws. Kiren overtook him, but he rose up and pushed back. This forced new energy to course through her.

"I guess I should thank you." Samantha let her eyes glow. There was no pain, only her anger. "You made me stronger than I ever was, but there's something you forgot."

"And what is that?" Michael spat in her ear.

"I was never yours." She pushed her power out from within herself as hard as she could. Michael soared through the air away from her. His tight grip on the blade handle ripped the dagger from her flesh. She dropped to her knees. Muscle, tendon, and skin knitted together instantly. She turned to face Michael, readying for his next attack, but she gasped at the sight before her. His body was flat against a broken piece of wall. Metal rods stuck out from his body at odd angles as his blood puddled on the floor.

His face twisted with fear. His eyes bulged as he gasped for air. He stared at her in disbelief before he closed his eyes and fell slack as the rods held him in place. Her breath caught in her throat as her stomach churned. She never wanted any of this to happen.

"Samantha!" A familiar voice shouted her name, snapping her out of her daze. She tore her eyes from Michael's body. Rhonda was holding Sebastion's arm over her shoulders. He was pale and had a deep cut on his side and leg that was gushing blood. Rhonda's lip was split, and her arm was bleeding. "We have to get out of here!" she yelled over the chaos going on around them. "The building's coming down."

"The tunnel," Sebastion said as he spat blood from his mouth. "It leads outside behind the warehouse. The entrance is back there." Sebastion pointed to an area that was full of rubble and debris.

"You two head that way. I have to get Deacon." Gunshots rang out behind them as bullets ricocheted in every direction.

"Okay." Sebastion moaned.

"Samantha, be careful." Rhonda squeezed her forearm as she helped Sebastion toward the location of the tunnel exit.

Samantha found Deacon and Kiren locked in battle. He was weakened by the powers she used on him earlier, but he was still putting up a good fight. They moved with heightened speed, as the moment seemed to slow down. Her heart beat fast and slow at the same time. Deacon was about to be flanked by the same green-eyed werewolf that went after Sebastion.

She ran as hard and as fast as she could to intercept him, but it was too late. Green Eyes grabbed Deacon around the throat as Kiren tore into him. She had to do something. If she forced them apart, he might snap Deacon's neck. She pushed out with her powers and shrouded them. The man holding Deacon let him go and dropped to one knee as he choked on silver and aconite.

Once she saw enough space between him and Deacon, she pushed Green Eyes far away from the fight. Before she could do the same to Kiren, he was pouncing on top of her. His full weight slammed into her, knocking them both to the ground. She tried to turn away from him, but she wasn't fast enough. His long, sharp fangs dug into her shoulder. She cried out in pain as he withdrew his teeth, tearing her skin as he did. She pushed him away as the green-eyed man came to his aid.

Kiren was choking on her blood as it ran down his chest. His thick veins stuck out through his tan skin as they darkened. Blood dripped onto the floor as he faced her. She expected him to be afraid, but he only smiled as they disappeared into the smoke that was quickly filling the building.

"Samantha!" Oscar shouted as he came to help Deacon to his feet. "My men are out, but we have to go. The building's going to explode. I saw gas drums on the way in. We must go now!"

"The tunnel," Deacon said in a weak voice as he pointed out the direction they should take. He was bleeding profusely and could barely stand on his own.

They ran toward the tunnel and spotted Sebastion and Rhonda already inside.

"Get in, quickly!" Samantha insisted. Oscar helped lower Deacon into the mouth of the dark tunnel. The first explosions erupted as werewolves and the rest of the hunters ran for their lives. Bodies were strewn across the floor in bloody heaps. Some were crushed under huge chunks of ceiling as others continued to fight rather than run.

"Samantha!" Oscar shouted to her from within the tunnel.

She tore her eyes from the carnage and dropped into the opening. She helped Oscar support Deacon's weight as they moved through the darkness. Lights mounted to the side walls lined their path, but most of the bulbs were out. The fire reached the gas drums as the building erupted. The explosion shook the tunnel, causing debris to shake loose from the ceiling.

"Go!" Samantha yelled at them. "Run!"

The group moved as fast as they could with their injuries.

"Almost there," she heard Sebastion wheeze. He was leaning a lot of weight on Rhonda. She grunted as she ran, but she didn't slow down.

Moonlight shone ahead of them, but there was a new problem. The explosion forced flames down into the tunnel. Fire licked the walls, and the heat charged toward them. Samantha turned just in time, creating a force field from within herself, pushing hard against the power of the flames. The brightness of it stung her eyes, and the heat evaporated the sweat on her brow.

"Move!" she yelled back at the group. "I don't know how long I can hold it." Her feet slid on the smooth dirt floor as she pushed with everything she had in her.

"We're not leaving you!" Rhonda yelled back.

"If you don't go, we all die down here. Go. Now!" she yelled as more debris fell from the ceiling.

Light shimmered off something on Samantha's shoulder as Oscar noticed the fang marks. The wound wasn't healing as dark blood gushed from the bite. Her new body mixing with the venom of an alpha would kill her. As he met Samantha's gaze, they realized she would not survive. He squeezed her good shoulder. "I'm so sorry." Tears gathered in his eyes. He turned away to push Sebastion and Rhonda forward. They yelled and fought to stay but inevitably moved further into the tunnel.

"I'm not leaving you." Deacon tried to stay on his

feet.

"You have to!" Samantha yelled at him over her shoulder. Blood began to run from her nose from the immense force she was exerting.

Deacon filled the space between them. The heat from the fire dried some of the blood that coated his skin. She was struggling to keep back the flames. The firelight danced off their faces as they met each other's eyes. "I'll stay with you." He wiped away the fresh blood from her nose.

"You have to live." The fire pushed hard against her force field. The exertion was quickly draining her strength.

He held her face. "I'm not leaving you." He held her gaze. "Never again."

Her chest ached as he leaned in to kiss her. She closed her eyes, and let his love pass through her until she was full of his essence. Her heart boomed in her chest under the strain. She pulled back from him as the kiss ended. "I love you. Always remember that I love you."

Deacon searched her face for any tell of what he could do to help her. He would do anything. Her eyes softened, and she smiled as she made her choice. Before he could react, she moved her right hand away from the fire and aimed it at him. "Forgive me," she said as she pushed him as far out of the tunnel as she could.

Painful sobs tore from her as the weight of the fire pushed hard against her power. Memories flashed in her mind as the tunnel grew quiet. A vision of her and Deacon playing together on the playground. Her parents' embrace calming her as they celebrated her graduation. Her father's hearty laughter echoing as he pushed her on the swing. The scent of vanilla, her mother's favorite perfume, filling her nose as if she were in the tunnel with her.

Her mind flashed over so many happy moments spent with Rhonda, and the hug she shared with Sebastion after finding out he was safe. Deacon's hands sliding over her shaking arms as if they were together again in Oscar's cabin. The memories filled her with so much joy she laughed as she cried. She might not have lived a long life, but at least it was filled with happy memories.

She opened her eyes and faced the fire. The heat evaporated the last of her tears. Kiren's bite burned through her body. His venom was hotter than the fire she was holding back. She hoped they reached safety as a thought crossed her mind. Living was sometimes harder than dying, but dying to save those you love was easy. She closed her eyes, and as a smile formed over her face, she dropped her hand, letting the flames consume her.

****

Deacon landed hard on the dirt floor of the tunnel after Samantha forced him away. The exit was a few feet behind him, but he couldn't leave. Dirt clung to his slick skin as he pushed himself from the ground. Every muscle in his body ached, and his head was spinning. He supported himself against the tunnel wall, but his strength was gone. He tried to go back to her but was stopped by Oscar.

"Deacon, she's gone!" he yelled at him as he fought to restrain him. "She's gone." His voice cracked as he tried to remain calm.

She couldn't be gone. He didn't want to live without her. She had to get out. If she kept moving, she'd be okay. His head was splitting as he willed her to live. He would see her again, he had to. The tightness in his chest stopped him from breathing. *This can't be happening.* His legs shook with every attempt to push against Oscar.

"Come on, son," Oscar said as he tried to keep himself from choking up. Oscar pulled him out of the tunnel and onto the wet grass just as flames exploded from its opening, sending dirt and debris everywhere.

Deacon's ears were ringing from the explosion as he got to his feet. The rain was pouring down on them as the flames receded within the tunnel. In the distance, sirens from emergency vehicles were heading their way. His stomach churned as the flames scorched the ground near them.

"They can't find us here, Deacon. We have to go now."

Deacon faced him with glowing eyes. "I can't just leave." His chest rose and fell with emotion.

"Sebastion is hurt bad. We have to go. He needs us now."

Sebastion was unconscious on the ground. Rhonda was cradling his head in her lap as she cried. His skin was pale, and his heartbeat was shallow. Samantha gave up her life to save them. He wouldn't let her sacrifice be in vain. Deacon and Oscar lifted Sebastion from the ground. They fled the scene just as flashing lights lit up the building. He stole a final glance at the tunnel before turning away. His heart shattered as if he had died instead.

Chapter 28

Days passed since the incident at the warehouse. Sebastion had to use crutches but was healing from the lacerations Eli gave him. Rhonda refused to leave his side as she and Oscar tended their wounds.

Deacon kicked some of the rubble scattered around the scarred remains of the warehouse. He kept to himself mostly since the incident. He checked in on Sebastion and brought him anything he needed, but he couldn't bear the way they looked at him whenever someone brought up Samantha. There was a wound within him that would never heal.

"Deac!" Sebastion shouted behind him as he tried to hobble his way over to him.

Deacon helped Sebastion steady himself as he viewed the cool overcast morning. "How's the leg?"

"Eh," Sebastion said as he lifted the boot he now had to wear. "It'll heal."

The sky was filled with pinks and reds that blended into dark purple and blue clouds. The ghostly image of a morning moon hung in the sky as it slowly dipped lower, leaving the heavens open for the sun to take its place.

"Deacon—" Sebastion concentrated as if couldn't find the words. "I'm sorry…about Samantha."

The remaining pieces of his heart crumbled at hearing her name. He would have to get used to her absence. Life went on no matter what, and he had to make himself realize that. He lost the love of his life twice in one lifetime, and part of him didn't want to recover.

"You ready to go?" Sebastion asked. "The funeral's starting soon."

"They never found her body," Deacon said. "How can they bury an empty box?"

"The fire would have—" Sebastion dropped his eyes to the ground. Deacon's pain radiated off him even though his face was blank. "Are you coming?"

"I can't believe she's really gone," Deacon admitted.

"I'll catch up with you later, then." Sebastion hobbled to where Rhonda was waiting with the car.

Deacon couldn't face Rhonda as he thought about the night they had here. Kiren and Eli escaped, but he doubted Kiren survived ingesting Samantha's blood. He wished that thought would've brought him relief, but he had a feeling that something worse was coming. They should have left Glenwood, but staying here made him feel he was still connected to her, and for now, that's what he needed.

****

The cemetery was full of people mourning the loss of so many from the warehouse explosion. It amazed Rhonda how many people showed up for Samantha. She spotted Bonnie. Today she wasn't wearing her brightly colored scrubs. Instead, she wore a black dress as she sat next to her husband and two daughters. She dabbed at her eyes with a tissue and shook her head with a steadying breath.

Jake still wore his employee shirt under a heavy, black jacket. He talked amongst the others that moved past him. Their coworkers and many of the patients they helped were in attendance. A tall woman stepped out of the crowd. She wore a black pantsuit and had long dark hair. She removed dark sunglasses and locked eyes with her. To her surprise, she thought the woman resembled Michael.

She quickly turned her head as she leaned toward Sebastion and Oscar who sat in front and beside her in the white, folding chairs the funeral home supplied them. "Does that woman look familiar to you?" she asked.

"What woman?" asked Sebastion as he searched the cemetery.

"Not so obvious, please! Oh no," Rhonda said as she noticed the woman move toward them. "She's coming this way."

As the woman walked over to them, she met her eyes and gave a small smile. "Hello," she said to the woman. "Did you know the deceased?" Words jumbled in her mind, but her anxiety twisted them around. She couldn't think of the right things to say.

"In a way." She tilted her head to the side and grinned. "My name's Jessica. Jessica McCray," she said as she shook each of their hands. "I'm Michael's sister. My brother and Miss Walker were together? Is that right?"

Rhonda nodded to Jessica. "I'm so sorry for your loss."

"Me too," Jessica said to them. "I won't keep you. I just thought I'd come over and introduce myself. I'm sure we'll be seeing more of each other."

"Do you live around here?" Oscar asked.

"I do now." With a nod, she left them as the preacher took his place by the grave. They glanced at each other before returning their sights to Jessica.

She faced them as she held open the door to a dark SUV. Her long dark hair swayed over her shoulder as she gave them a slow, knowing grin. With that, she was gone.

"We're in trouble," Rhonda said as she turned back toward the ceremony.

"She might not be involved," Oscar whispered.

"You know she is," Sebastion blurted. "Why else would she walk over here and say what she said?"

"We'll check into it. For now, we're here for a funeral." Oscar turned in his seat and adjusted his jacket.

Rhonda, Sebastion, and Oscar breathed a heavy sigh and watched as they lowered an empty coffin into the ground.

****

It was weeks before Deacon could visit her grave. The mourners were long gone, and all the white chairs were removed from the Black Woods Cemetery. He walked across the hallowed ground, reading the different names from each gravestone as he passed. Some were blank from erosion. He waited patiently for the gravediggers to finish their job of filling a nearby grave before moving any closer. They loaded their equipment and left through the cemetery gate. The small funeral home sat in the distance, shrouded in mist.

A small white cross marked Samantha's grave until the headstone was delivered. His breath fogged as he sighed. The temperature dropped in the past week. Winter was setting in on Glenwood. A few snowflakes drifted from the cloudy sky before they settled on the frozen ground.

He pulled his jacket tight around him as the wind

blew, sending a chill through to his bones. Memories of Samantha filled his mind. He loved her and always would. He wondered how long his heart would ache like it did. He just got her back, when he lost her again, for good this time.

Tears stung his eyes, but he wouldn't let them fall. He kept his emotions bottled up within himself. It was hard to breathe under the strain of them. Releasing what he carried in his chest would help, but if he did, then that would mean he was ready to accept she was truly gone. Every night he woke up, and for a glorious moment, he thought she survived. His suffering would be endless, or at least until he joined her in death.

The cemetery, like most areas of Glenwood, was lined with thick forests. Twigs snapped somewhere in the distance where the cemetery grass merged with the tree line. He turned his head toward the sound, expecting to see a deer or some other woodland creature, but there was nothing there.

The ghosts of the dead had risen to watch him as he mourned. Another gust of wind blew through him. Leaves were lifted from the ground as they swirled in the drift before returning to the dirt. He caught a familiar scent, but he didn't dare to let himself believe it was her. His mind recalled her memory, and that's what brought the scent to him.

Another twig snapped in the distance, but this time, it was closer. He searched the area. His grief was playing tricks on him. His breath quickened as he followed the tree line with his eyes. Jutting out from the trees a few feet above the ground, Deacon spotted a large, flat rock, and standing on top was a black wolf. Its deep hazel eyes were trained on him as the winter breeze ruffled strands of its dark fur.

He couldn't tear his eyes from the sight as another gust of wind washed over him, carrying her scent. He closed his eyes and breathed deeply, allowing it to fill him. It warmed his body, and a sliver of hope bloomed in his tight chest. The wolf was gone when he opened his eyes.

"Samantha?" he asked the emptiness as he thought to himself. *She's alive!*

Epilogue

Eli trudged slowly through the fallen bodies of his pack. A lot of them escaped but succumbed to the wounds they received during the fight. He was summoned by Kiren, since the heat from the warehouse incident had died down. There were losses on all sides that night. The death toll was higher than he expected. The farther into the old mansion he got, the more he could smell the stench of death permeating its walls.

Kiren was gravely infected from the blood he had ingested after marking Samantha. He was healing but at a much slower rate. It alarmed Eli to see more of his brethren dead at his feet as he walked through the crumbling remains of Kiren's hideout. Some of their throats were ripped out so savagely they were decapitated.

"I see you got my message." He heard Kiren's voice up ahead in the dark.

"I came as soon I could," he said as he drew nearer to his alpha. His back was to him until his approach made him turn.

"Good, good," Kiren said as he stepped into the light.

Blackened blood had dried under Kiren's nostrils, but his attention was quickly drawn to the fresh blood on his claws. His heart jumped into his throat as each crimson drop hit the floor. "Is this why you needed so many in the pack? You planned to kill them to help you survive her infection?" he asked in an angry tone, but Kiren didn't respond.

"Have you heard the news?" Kiren asked his only remaining beta. He pointed to a small table and a newspaper that sat on top of its scarred wooden surface.

Eli walked over and ran his hand over the cover photo. He turned his wide eyes to him. "So, it did work? She survived."

"As I knew she would," Kiren said through raspy breaths as he moved toward him.

Eli surveyed the carnage. "What happened?" He gestured around them.

"We needed a fresh start," Kiren said coldly as he wrapped a bloody hand around Eli's throat and squeezed. "Wouldn't you agree?"

Eli nodded as Kiren's grip slowly cut off his air supply. His claws threatened to puncture his flesh.

"Good." Kiren spoke as he released him and moved back toward the table that held the newspaper. "We must hurry. There's a lot to be done." He peered over his shoulder as he flashed his ghoulish eyes. "We'll have our queen soon."

"How can you be sure she'll come to you?" Eli asked. "We saw how it turned out for the hunter that tried to control her."

"I don't plan to control her," Kiren stated. "I plan to be the one on her side, dropping a kind and understanding word here and there in her ear. I'll help her grow into her new abilities. I won't have to *make* her do anything. In time, she will come to me of her own free will."

Kiren read the article's headline, "MISSING GIRL

PRESUMED DEAD HAS BEEN FOUND!" Underneath the headline was a photo of Samantha. An emergency blanket wrapped around her and at her side was Deacon.

"Besides," Kiren said with a snarl as he laid a bloodied hand over the photograph before he crumpled it in his claws. "I'm her alpha now."

A word about the author…

Tashia Fugate lives in Kentucky with her husband where the town may be small, but the people are mighty and it's where she calls home. When she's not reading or walking, she enjoys painting, crafting, music and letting her imagination off its leash with her writing.

From the time Tashia was in high school then to college and off into the work force she's been a dreamer. She is always inventing characters and new places for their adventures to take place. She's more than excited to bring those adventures to her readers with her first book. Enjoy!

www.ingramcontent.com/pod-product-compliance
Lightning Source LLC
Chambersburg PA
CBHW070309040726
47501CB00018B/1278